Koenig slid down the Command Cabin emergency chute and came down ankle deep in the warm sand of Megaron. From every angle there was a black, uniformed figure walking forward, closing in a circle. Koenig addressed himself to the burly character who seemed to be the leader.

"We are from Moonbase Alpha. We come in peace—but we were forced to defend ourselves. We are seeking a place to live."

The leader's eyes had a blank, fanatical look; probably he listened closely only to himself.

He said, "You have killed many of my people. You will stand trial. Spadec will decide what is to be done with you!"

Books in the Space: 1999 Series

Published by POCKET BOOKS

PHOENIX OF MEGARON

JOHN RANKINE

PUBLISHED BY POCKET BOOKS NEW YORK

PHOENIX OF MEGARON

Futura Publications edition published 1976

POCKET BOOK edition published November, 1976

POCKET BOOK editions are published by
POCKET BOOKS,
a division of Simon & Schuster, Inc.
A GULF+WESTERN COMPANY
630 Fifth Avenue,
New York, N.Y. 10020.
Trademarks registered in the United States
and other countries.

ISBN: 0-671-80764-1.

Printed in the U.S.A.

PHOENIX OF
MEGARON

CHAPTER ONE

No one coming out to Moonbase Alpha on a routine duty stint could have imagined that they were stepping from the Eagle shuttle onto the surface of a nuclear bomb, primed and ready to go.

The great, sprawling base, with its complement of over three hundred hand-picked specialists, was a well-found ship. Except for the view of a stark moon-scape from the direct-vision ports, the personnel could forget they were out on a fragile limb, with only the hurrying Eagles to link them to Earth Planet.

When the mass of nuclear waste, dumped in the disposal pits, hit a threshold and erupted in a savage discharge, the link was snapped. Earth's ancient partner was booted out of orbit and sent naked and alone on an interstellar odyssey, where the strange was commonplace and the writ of Earth-based logic no longer ran.

Commander John Koenig found himself captain of a rudderless hulk. They were adrift in a wilderness beyond the grasp of imagination. But against all reason, he held doggedly to the conviction that, somewhere, there was a planetfall waiting to be made. Somewhere, he would bring his people to a new Earth.

Moontime, it was sixteen hundred hours on the nose. John Koenig sat in his command office and drummed on his desk top with a stylus. Of all the times of the Moon day, it was the one for nostalgia. By the calendar, though it meant nothing to the stark, changeless moonscape, it was late November. He remembered how it would be in northern cities on Earth Planet. Street lights in a magenta glow, before the tubes warmed to full daylight simulation; houses and stores already lit. It had always seemed a magical time, when a turn of the next corner would start something new and unexpected.

He left his desk and walked over to the direct-vision port, a tall, powerful figure, hawk faced, black hair cropped neatly. The unexpected was out there, all right. If the long journey had taught anything, it was that fact was a stranger animal than fiction. Any one of the myriad stars, scattered like jewels on a velvet cloth, might hold a people whose life style was on the outer edge of credibility.

The *Voyager* tapes had given chapter and verse for that. Golden ant men on Chrysaor. Reptilean killers on the dying world of Scotia. Urbane, silvery, mandarin types on Fingalna. They were well off the track for all those worlds. But the iron laws of probability dictated that there would be others like them.

The scale was too vast. Still vaguely restless, he shoved down a stud on his console and the screen that divided him from Main Mission rolled silently aside. The senior operations team was at the end of the first dog watch and ready to stand down. Paul Morrow, Main Mission controller, was taking his deputy through the log. Sandra Benes, systems analyst and communications expert, moved elegantly aside to allow Leanne to take the desk. A sleek, dark head and a spectacular fair one were leaned together in a tableau. Alan Carter had already vacated the Eagle Command desk and was talking to Kano, whose relief at the computer spread was overdue.

Koenig felt the contrast. Outside, the scale was too inhuman to grasp. Inside, it was too small. For all the purposeful work that went on and kept life going on Alpha, they were only going through the motions of living. They needed a break. Most of all, they needed space, elbow room, somewhere to go when the watch went below.

Quietly, he closed the screen and used his comlock to open the hatch. Locked in their private conversations, Main Mission staff hardly noticed him as he strode through and went on into one of the main throughways of the sprawling complex. Still thoughtful, he reckoned there was the loneliness of the trackless outback where the Moon was a rambling dust mote, and there was the loneliness that every man carried round in his own head. Each living thing was an atoll and few craft beat a path over the reefs.

Victor Bergman, scientific adviser to the Base, lifted his head from a littered workbench as Koenig came through the hatch of his projects lab. Balding and grizzled, with the high dome forehead of a thinker, he seemed to suffer less than most from the long constraint of life in Alpha. One lab was much like another to him and he reckoned he could shake a catalyptic concept out of the woodwork as well there as anywhere. But he was glad to see the top hand. His lined face split into a characteristic grin.

"John. Social call or business?"

"Does it make a difference?"

Bergman slid away a panel in the front of his workbench and pulled out a long-necked bottle and a couple of glasses. "Hydroponics have been working on a liqueur for special occasions. They sent a sample for official approval."

"Let's say 'social,' then."

"I'm glad you said that. This is the time of day when alcohol fortifies the mind."

Koenig took a cautious sip. The hydroponics team were enthusiasts, but asbestos throated to the last man. This time, they had a winner. Golden in the beaker, it was smooth as silk with a lingering afterglow.

"Is it safe to ask what they put in it?"

"All good stuff. Sugar. Honey simulate, citric acid, cold tea, mace, cloves, ginger, yeast, raisins. It's all on the manifest."

Koenig sat on the bench and considered his friend. "You keep on an even keel, Victor. What's the secret?"

"There's always work to do."

"A therapy in itself."

"So they say. You should know. You work harder than anybody on this base."

"What's the current project?"

"Small stuff. I'm supposing that a first problem, when we find a planet, will be a power supply. We can't use the Eagles forever. I've been thinking about the scale of operations. I believe we should stay small. Small communities. Most of the ills on Earth Planet came from too many people in units that were too big."

"It'll be many generations before we have a population problem."

"True, but we should lay down the guidelines from the beginning. We should go for methods and equipment that leave room for human creativity."

"Labour-intensive industry, not overmuch mechanisation?"

"It's right, when you think about it."

"How do you ever get the sort of productive know-how that could mount a space programme?"

"You have to decide whether a space programme is all that vital."

"Now, that's something I never expected to hear from a professor of astrophysics."

"Where did it get Earth Planet in the end? Or ourselves, for that matter. Earth was choking itself with atomic waste. It doesn't solve any human problems."

"You're not saying there were no human problems in the early days, when the only nut grew on a tree? As I recall, Cain was beating Abel over the head, when there was freehold land for the asking and no taxes."

Bergman shifted his ground, relishing the argument and putting forward another pet theory. "Work has to be seen to have an end product. Things can get too impersonal. Organisations can get too big. What could you reckon was the ideal size for a city?"

"It needs to be big enough to afford some public architecture. Big enough to give protection, fall-back benefits, culture, choices. You could make a list. At least a hundred thousand, I'd say."

"I think you'd be close at that."

Koenig sipped his drink. Bergman set up an open-topped canister, cleared a litter of gear from the work-bench and switched on a miniature fan.

Koenig said, "No problem, then. How long before an Alphan colony hits a hundred thousand?"

"But the foundations have to be right. As the sapling is bent, so will the tree grow."

"I can't disagree with that. What's the model?"

"A Yen Tornado Tower. It's an old idea that Grumman Aerospace worked on. It was never taken up as it should have been. It could generate a million watts from a turbine only two metres across. All for free."

"Given a prevailing wind."

"Wrong. It doesn't matter which way the wind blows. Watch."

Bergman threw a switch. There was a subdued hum from his canister and a spread of small telltales lit up. He shifted the fan, taking it round three hundred and sixty degrees, so that it blew on the device from every direction. As he moved around, slits opened in succession to take in the airstream. There was no loss of power.

"That's very smart, Victor. How does it work?"

"There's a turbine on a vertical axis at the bottom. Open top, as you see. Wind blows in through an open vane, spirals to the centre and creates a vortex. Pressure at the centre is reduced. There's a big pressure gradient between the centre and the top airstream flowing over. Air gets sucked in from ducts below the turbine blades."

"An updated windmill?"

"Easier to build than a conventional windmill; smaller, more efficient power conversion. Easy to build. Easy to service."

"One for every homestead?"

"Why not?"

Koenig thought about it. Windmills could be serviced by a village craftsman. Turbines and generators needed a back-up supply chain. Not as complex, however, as the atomic power plant that kept Alpha's life-support systems at the bubble. It was good intermediate technology. Both men were absorbed in the discussion and the communications post buzzed twice before Koenig surfaced.

It was Leanne, trying to copy Sandra's precise, unhurried manner, but unable to keep excitement out of her voice. "Main Mission calling Commander Koenig."

"Koenig."

"It's a contact, Commander."

"Don't let it go away. I'll be there. Alert executive personnel."

Victor Bergman switched off his demonstration. They looked at each other across the bench. It was all beginning again.

Koenig said, "Keep your fingers crossed, Victor. In twelve months, we could be looking for a draughty corner for one of your towers."

There was a full set of Alphan top brass to see Sandra Benes make a final, delicate tuning ploy and drop a small blue and white sphere on the centre of the big screen.

Helena Russell, executive of medical services on Alpha and Koenig's apple, turned quickly from a monitor spread. *"Definite* life signs, John. Too early to be sure, but I'd say on a human scale."

There was more encouragement from Kano's computer. He tore a print out from the outfall and handed it to Bergman. "Looks good, Professor."

All eyes were on the expert as he scanned down the list and made a racing summary. He said slowly, "This must be one of the best prospects we've had, John."

There was a reservation and Koenig was on to it. "But there's something you're not sure of . . . ."

"I'll come to that. On the credit side, we have a troposphere with a breathable atmosphere, four parts inert gas and one part oxygen. There's a protective ozone layer about thirty kilometres up. Soaks up radiation. Progressive thinning of atmosphere density to six hundred kilometres. Layered like Earth Planet. Conditions would be roughly similar. Thirty percent land masses. Seventy percent oceans. There's every chance evolution might follow the same pattern, give or take a few variations. Gravity at sea level within half a percent of Earth's, so the biological scale would be the same."

Koenig said, "That's the good news. What's the reservation?"

"As I see it, we take a tangential course at the extreme limit of the gravisphere. It's a question of whether we go close enough to get a reconnaissance team down and back and then mount Operation Exodus."

Koenig reckoned bitterly that it figured. The odds against pulling an Earth type planet out of the cosmic hat were mind bending. The odds against finding such a one on a convenient course, so that they could investigate it at leisure and then step over to it from their life raft, were too high to calculate. He said, "Work on it, Victor. Command conference in one hour. We'll look at every fact we can stack together. Try to raise them, Sandra. If there's a high-level culture over there, somebody will be looking at us. Let's have no mistakes about intentions."

Sandra said, "Check, Commander," and swivelled away to get on with it. As Koenig left the floor for his command office, her message was already on the way.

"This is Moonbase Alpha. We come in peace, seeking your help. We have travelled from the planet Earth. We seek a place to live."

She stopped and keyed in a prepared transmission from Computer. If the receiving station was equipped to handle it, there were data in a mathematical form which would build up a stylised picture of a man and a woman and a potted history of human evolution.

On the big screen, the blue and white planet was unchanged. If there was anybody at home, they were not answering the bell. But, on the credit side, there was no strike force arrowing out to defend its corner of space. Sandra started over: "This is Moonbase Alpha. We come in peace. . . ."

When Koenig assembled his senior executives round the conference table in the command office, there was still no response. Helena Russell could confirm life signs and pinpoint them to three widely separated areas, but whoever was down there, looking up at their sky, was making no sign.

Koenig said, "I don't have to tell you what the chances are of finding this kind of planet. Helena confirms that there's everything we need to support life. But before we get too steamed up about it, we'll hear Victor."

Victor Bergman was not looking too happy. He had no relish for being the one with the knocking copy. He shuffled his papers and ran his fingers through his thinning hair. He said, "I confirm Doctor Russell's report. This planet is the best yet, but unfortunately we pass at extreme Eagle range. There would be time for an Eagle to get there, make one, single orbit, make a selected planetfall for one hour and get back. After that, no dice. If we waited for a reconnaissance Eagle to bring back data, the time for decision would be past. We *can* send an Eagle, on a tight time schedule, and I'd say it might be worthwhile. For one thing, hydroponics could use some fresh, vigorous plant strains for protein synthesis. That and other sampling data would pay for a visit. But on the main count, I don't see how we can mount Operation Exodus in the time."

Paul Morrow said, "We have a lot of data and it all looks good. We could decide on that. Operation Exodus could be a reconnaissance in strength."

It was faster than Koenig wanted to go. He said, "There's no denying the temptation to pack up and move out. God knows, it's what we all want. But not at any price. If we keep our nerve, we have a guaranteed life here for many years yet. To some extent, we can afford to choose. We shouldn't throw it away on a blind chance——"

Impulsively, Alan Carter broke in: "Not blind, Commander. We know a lot about the planet and it's all good."

Koenig was not to be stampeded. He said, "You know and I know, Alan, that what looks good from Main Mission can turn sour on the ground. I could not authorise Operation Exodus without a surface reconnaissance. The question is, how detailed should that reconnaissance be? Professor Bergman gives us one orbit. Perhaps ten hours, overall. Suppose we used all that time for a landing, close to a centre of population? It's possible we could make contact and come to a decision. Operation Exodus could be ready to go. Instead of the Eagle making the return trip, the Eagle fleet would be on the move and part way home."

Helena said, "And if it was negative?"

"The Eagle would signal to abort the mission. There would be time for the fleet to get back. It would not cross the halfway line without a signal to come on."

"If there was no signal?"

"No signal would read as negative. Abort the mission."

"And the Eagle would be written off?"

Koenig said steadily, "And the Eagle would be written off."

Helena Russell knew for a truth who would command the ship and went suddenly silent.

There was not much comment to be had. Sandra Benes looked across the circle to Paul Morrow. Like Helena, she had an emotional stake in who was to crew the reconnaissance ship.

Long experience told Koenig how to read the silence. Nobody liked working to such a narrow margin, but given the situation, there was no other way to play it. He said, "Well then, it's a question of logistics. Phase One for Operation Exodus can start as of now.

Controlled shutdown of all sections. Load the Eagles. Leave Alpha ready for reoccupation. Phase Two begins when the probe Eagle reaches the gravisphere of the planet. The Eagle fleet leaves Alpha. Phase Three is triggered by report data from the Eagle, allowing a maximum of six hours from the beginning of Phase Two. It has two possibilities. Continue to a designated landing area or backtrack and return to Alpha. Here and now, I put it on the line as a command decision: Phase Three is only confirmed by my signal. The absence of such a signal is negative. In the absence of a direct confirmation, the fleet must return. Is that clear?"

He looked round the table.

"Kano?"

"Agreed, Commander."

"Paul?"

"Agreed."

"Sandra?"

"Agreed, Commander. But should there not be some backup help for the reconnaissance party?"

"If an armed Eagle can't handle it, we should be wasting more lives and resources. The answer has to be no. Victor?"

"Given the circumstances, the plan is logical."

"Helena?"

"I don't like it, but I have to agree. Certainly, the planet seems to offer the best chance we have had so far."

"Alan?"

Alan Carter lifted two thumbs for good measure. "Ready to go, Commander."

"Then it remains for me to detail the Eagle crew." Koenig switched in the auto log and made it formal. "It has to be small. Since the final decision is mine, I shall command and act as navigator. Pilot, Captain Carter. Scientific assessment, Professor Bergman. Two security men. Rufford and Jansen. Command of Alpha and Operation Exodus devolves on Controller Morrow. Any questions?"

Helena Russell tried. "Medical assessment. I should go along."

"Not necessary. We already have a clear on medical data. You are needed on Alpha."

Carter said, "Eagle Seven is the stand-by, armed Eagle. She can be ready for extended flight within the hour."

"Eagle Seven it is, then."

Moonbase Alpha slipped easily into top gear. It was the payoff for all the emergency drills and the planning that had gone into the Operation Exodus file. Koenig was more than satisfied. Even after the longest duty stint that any space farers had ever endured, he still had a taut ship. It was going by the book.

At a personal level, there was more of a problem. Helena Russell seemed to be keeping out of his way. The countdown clock in his head was beating round for Eagle Seven's lift-off and she was nowhere to be found. He tried to be honest with himself and decide whether he had kept her out of the crew on a personal kick, to keep her safe, or whether it was the greatest good of the greatest number that had pushed him to a decision.

Even when he was in the travel tube, sealed up in space gear and moving to launch pad seven, he was still mulling it over and no nearer a final answer. But she had successfully avoided him and he had to make a positive effort of will to clear her out of his mind and concentrate on the mission.

Carter and the security details were already aboard. Victor Bergman, knowing his friend's mind, said, "It's not Helena's style to hold a grudge, John. She knows you were right. She'll be the first with a goodwill message, when we get under way. Exodus makes heavy demands on Medicentre staff. She has her hands full."

It was no more than Koenig had been thinking, but it was still no substitute for a personal leave-taking. In Eagle Seven, Carter was already working through prelift-off checks. Bergman went through into the passenger module. Koenig dropped into the copilot seat beside Carter and snapped down his visor. Paul Morrow's face appeared on the scanner. "Main Mission to Eagle Seven. You are clear for lift-off."

Carter said, "All systems go. Counting."

Koenig felt the familiar surge of excitement in his circuits. Before all else, he was a spacefarer. Admin was a second role, which he did because he had been cast for it. The rising beat of Eagle Seven's motors chimed with his mood. Moondust churned past the direct-vision ports and the ship jacked herself off her pad like a free-standing elevator. He began to call course data to the pilot.

Watchers in Main Mission saw Eagle Seven hover half a kilometre above the base, turn to pick up a course and arrow away. Sandra had them on the scanner with the blue and white planet as a backdrop. She put a variant in her transmission. "This is Moonbase Alpha. We come in peace. The ship approaching your planet contains our leader, Commander John Koenig. There is no danger to you. We ask that you should meet him and hear what he has to say."

The halls and covered ways of Alpha were thronged with orderly lines of Alphans as Phase One of Operation Exodus began to bite. Faces were serious. It had happened before and there had been disappointments. Most were treating it as yet another training exercise, but there was a question mark in every head. Was this the one? Had they finally gotten to the end of the line?

Aboard Eagle Seven, the hours peeled away. Koenig shrugged out of his harness and snapped open the seals on his visor. On-board computers had it sorted. Eagle Seven could fly herself, a bobbin on a string. It was time to relax and see what Rufford had managed to cook up in the miniature galley. His hand was on the hatch release to open up the passenger module, when the panel slid away. Framed in the gap was a bulky, space-suited figure, balancing a tray on one hand, which showed high-level motor control, even allowing for the Eagle's gravity simulator.

It was also a peace offering. The eyes behind the visor were part of the furniture of his mind. Helena Russell said, "Don't blame Rufford, John. I told him it was a change of plan. He had no choice. I know it wasn't fair, but I had to come along."

Koenig backed off and allowed her through. She set coffee and sandwiches beside Carter. He was more forthcoming. "Doctor Russell! Great stuff. I'm glad the commander changed his mind. Charm might do more good than diplomacy down there."

Koenig took his rations in silence. He could have said, "Look. What you've done makes a nonsense of command. You're a senior executive. If you go your own way, how can you expect any crewman to follow orders? There has to be one voice or the whole shooting match falls apart."

To some extent, she was waiting for it, twisting the tray nervously and mad at herself for feeling like a junior about to be balled out by a consultant for leaving a swab in an abdominal cavity. She was as surprised as he was when he said, "How can I say anything, except that I'm glad to have you aboard?"

In fact, the mildness of it was a more telling rebuke than anything else he could have said. She turned away, unable to answer.

Koenig joined them in the passenger module, drank his coffee and watched the blue and white planet expand slowly in the direct-vision port. It was possible to see something of the land-mass distribution. Each pole had a dark, irregular cap. Then there was a broad belt of ocean. The equator had an archipelago of great continents, strung like beads on a chain. It would make for broadly similar conditions. Except for the polar regions, there would be no extremes of climate.

Victor Bergman theorised, "All the equatorial land is close enough for interchange of populations. Wherever civilisations started, they'd soon be in contact. By this time you'd expect a single, homogeneous race of people."

It was Helena's subject and she reckoned she could not stay silent and contrite forever. "But it would depend on how far development went, before they began to spread around. There could be as many ethnic types as we have on Earth Planet."

"But it's the climate that makes surface changes. Subcutaneous fat gives an Eskimo a different face. Underneath, he's blood brother to a lean and angular Apache."

"True for that; but you can't explain away cephalic indices. Round head, long head, that's not climate."

Relayed from Carter's instrument spread, Paul Morrow's voice joined them. "Main Mission calling Eagle Seven. Come in, Eagle Seven."

Carter answered, "Eagle Seven. What is it, Paul?"

"This will be the last transmission from Moonbase Alpha. All sections closed down. Eagle fleet assembled and ready to go. Phase Two, Operation Exodus beginning in three minutes.

Carter called through, "Did you get that, Commander? Any word for Alpha?"

The operation was running like a machine, but it was still on a track with no visible end. Koenig said shortly, "No comment. We have no further information."

Carter softened it. "I read you, Paul. Say good-bye to Alpha for me. No change. The planet still looks good. Keep in touch."

Helena Russell could imagine the scene in Main Mission, lights dimmed, consoles silent, the hatch closing behind Morrow and Sandra Benes as they went to join the last Eagle. It had been home for a long time and in spite of the hazards, it had treated them well. They had all grown in stature and understanding. Few communities, anywhere, could have learned to live together so well. It should stand them in good stead when they came to establish their colony. On the other hand, once the pressures were off and life could go on, even without mutual support and cooperation, there could be a change. There was something to be said for an external threat. Facing a common enemy kept small differences in perspective. Politicians through the ages had known about that one. There was nothing like a war to unite people behind the government, and a constant battle against an environment that was as hostile as it could get was tailor made. It would all depend on Koenig and the lead he gave from the beginning. She was about to join him and share this seminal thought, when it occurred to her that her action in rocking the boat was not a good start. It would be wiser to wait.

Victor Bergman broke into her reverie. "Helena. What do you make of this?"

He had set up his own data-acquisition network with an independent computer to process the take. The printout he handed over to her was an analysis of radiation levels on the central land mass of the continental chain. It was the first setback, and the implications were clear.

Helena said, "It's a classic picture. There was an atomic incident. Epicentre, fallout. All a long time ago. Except for a small area, these levels are acceptable."

"Long term?"

"There has always been radiation, from the Earth itself and from the Sun. The human race tolerates it, up to a point."

"This looks like a local source."

"And we have to ask whether it was natural or man made."

Koenig had joined them and took the paper from her. He read it in silence, then he handed it to Bergman. "Check all the land you can reach. What about life signs?"

Helena said, "Still strong in some seaboard areas."

Carter took a spell. He walked through the passenger module to chat up Jansen in the rumble. Koenig plotted a course that would take Eagle Seven in a descending spiral and smooth out in an orbit to the north of the zero latitude line. It would cross sea and land and take in many maritime zones, where the specialists said there were life signs. In his mind's eye, he could see the Eagle armada strung out over the star map. Already, some of the gloss was off the enterprise. Nothing ever remained straightforward for long. With even low-level radiation, there was the long-term genetic danger. The race, still batting on the surface, could well be mutated out of their five wits. He was even more sure that he had been right to insist on close reconnaissance. He called Morrow. "Eagle Seven to Eagle Fleet Command."

Sandra Benes, with her usual flair for meticulous detail, tuned herself onto the scanner, composed on the Golden Section, expressive eyes like pools of chocolate milk. "Eagle Fleet to Eagle Seven, I read you."

"Koenig. Put me over to Paul on a one to one."

There was no sense in spreading doubt at this stage. On a closed link to Morrow's ear there would be no general transmission on the net. Paul Morrow's face replaced Sandra's. Aesthetically it was no gain, but Koenig knew his man. Paul Morrow was rock steady in any kind of crisis.

"Commander?"

"Any problems?"

"None. All personnel in good shape. Right on schedule.

"Keep a low profile on this one. Nothing definite, but Victor has data on radiation. Still viable, but it makes for reservations. This is a one-off exercise and it has to be right."

"I read you."

"No hesitation at halfway house. There's nothing spare on the clock."

"I know it, Commander."

"Good luck, then."

"One thing, Commander. Doctor Russell is with you?"

"That's right. She convinced me against my will.

But maybe she was right. Her opinion on this radiation will be decisive."

"Good luck to you, then."

Heat shields on Eagle Seven were beginning to show signs of thermal agitation. They were moving into the extreme, etiolated layers of the planet's atmosphere. Carter returned to the command cabin and Koenig moved over to the navigation slot. He spoke on the intercom to the passenger module. "Time to seal up. I'm closing the hatch. We do one orbit. Keep the data coming."

The hatch sliced shut at his back. Jansen unlocked the swivel of his gunnery island and made a three-sixty-degree turn with his hands on the firing grips of the stern lasers.

Sensors shoved out a record of outside temperature: fifteen hundred Celsius, through a golden glow of charged solar particles; a gradual drop to one thousand and the spectacle of a multihued aurora; five hundred and Bergman was clocking a band of almost pure oxygen. There was a rapid shift to minus sixty, through a freak layer of heavy particles, and Eagle Seven was falling through the ionosphere.

Now there was more to see. Main geographical features could be picked out. Mountain ranges, plains, the run of major rivers and a hint of colour. Temperature dropped again through a cold layer of ozone; dropped again to clock minus sixty and then pulled back to an even zero as Carter levelled out a kilometre over the highest peaks.

Koenig called the expert. "Any comment so far, Victor?"

Bergman was doing his best to keep his voice level and judicial, but there was no mistaking the satisfaction in it. "Sea-level temperatures around twenty-two Celsius. A Mediterranean climate, John. An orangery in every backyard."

"And every orange radioactive."

Helena heard it on the net and came in. "Not so, John. The radiation levels are tolerable. There's heavier screening from solar radiation and less natural build up. We believe there were local atomic events, but way back."

"You're saying conditions will get better and, in fact, they're reasonable as of now?"

"Right."

Carter sheered off from the mountain range and dropped lower, over a coastal strip edged with white lace, where the wine-dark sea pounded into shingle and sand beaches. He said, "Where have all the people gone, Commander?"

Answer came as he went lower again and the landscape was peeling away below the hurrying Eagle. Helena Russell's awed voice breathed over the intercom: "Only look at that, John!"

Jacking itself up over the horizon was a pentagon of immense towers. When it was all plain to see, the scale was enormous. Five tower blocks, each verging on two-kilometres high, were set round a circle to mark the limits of a five-pointed star. At ground level, the design was carried out in pale-green translucent walls. The beaches were empty because the people had gathered themselves together in one place. It spoke of strong government and positive planning. It also spoke of a level of culture where communication with a wandering asteroid would be no sweat.

Alarm bells sounded in Koenig's head. He was expecting interceptor craft to streak out and cut them down. Then he was staring at the nearer tower and the answer was plain. A jagged fissure ran two-thirds of its height. There would be no attack. They were in tumbleweed country and passing a ghost town.

Carter said formally, "Do I land, Commander?"

Koenig had the answer ready. "No. We go on. There's no time. We land if and when we can talk to people. We need to know what goes on."

Eagle Seven's angular shadow fled on. There was no challenge. Spaced out along the seaboard, the silent, empty cities of the planet were dumb shells. Whoever had built them had long gone.

She crossed a wide strip of brilliant blue sea and began again over another continent. This time the pattern of building changed. It was still on a mind-bending scale, but the ground plan was less regular. There was evidence of harbour works and in one, a massive freighter was lifted out of the sea and chocked at a crazy angle against the foot of a tower block.

Helena called the top hand. "John, radiation levels are right down. This is A-okay."

Before he could answer, Carter had something else on the forward probes. "Commander!"

Koenig checked it out. The scanner had it plain. By comparison with what they had seen, it was a very small city, set on a peninsula between two river estuaries. But there was movement. Gnatlike air cars were rising from every quarter. Somebody at last had gotten on to the notion that there was an intruder approaching the hive.

CHAPTER TWO

Eagle Seven was diving out of the sun like a stooping falcon. She could cut a swathe through the rising air cars before their pilots knew what was happening. Carter had the main lasers locked on and was waiting for the good word with his hands on the grips.

It would be no way to start a peace mission. Koenig said, "Steady as you go, Captain. Once across. Turn. Come in slowly and hover over the control square."

Meanwhile, he used all the power he had on the communications net to send out a signal on fourteen twenty, coupled with a simultaneous audio repeat from the outside P.A. system. His voice reverberated round the city.

"This is Commander John Koenig. We come from the moon which has appeared in your sky. We ask for permission to land in your city and talk with you. We come in peace."

Eagle Seven turned, still falling. Some of the leading air cars had the height of her and Carter looked dubious as he began the return leg. There was no answer from the ground. Seen closer, the cars had a black and silver finish which gave them the look of police tenders. They had formed into three squadrons. One was wheeling to keep station above the Eagle; one was deploying to box her in, port and starboard; the third was holding off, ready to support. There was no doubt —they were working a classic manoeuvre to force her down.

A single car peeled off the higher flight and bore in. Even before a succession of hammer blows thumped along the superstructure, Koenig had read the message. He called, "Jansen. Fire as you bear." An eye-aching thread seared out from Eagle Seven's stern module and the air car was instant scrap, falling in a plume of black smoke.

Koenig called urgently, "If you attack, we are forced to defend. Do not attack. We have no wish to use our power."

It was all strictly for the birds. Either the pilots were suicide bent to a man, or they were brainwashed into a death-or-glory stance. They came in from every quarter. Eagle Seven was shuddering along her length, and although her destructive power was away and beyond anything the cars could put out, it was only a matter of time before the sheer volume of small fire carried away some key structures.

Koenig said, "Out. As fast as you like."

Carter threw every gramme of urge into a crash lift and the Eagle clawed herself up in a spectacular thrust. There was a check that strained them against their harness and a grinding jar that sent a ripple through the fabric. The damage-report panel threw up a rash of red hatchings. An air car had finally gotten itself through Jansen's destructive guard. Flaming like a torch, it was jammed definitively between the upper rocket tubes. Jansen's module was a shattered wreck and the security man was pinned to his swivel chair by the rapier antenna on the car's snub cone.

Eagle Seven was falling. Carter fought the failing gear every metre of the way, pulled them half a kilometre out of the city, brought her down at a crazy angle on the slope of a sand dune, beside a wide estuary. Hover cars dropped around them in a circle.

Bitterly, Koenig considered the communications console. Acrid smoke wreathed the panel. It was a write-off. The only element of satisfaction left to him was the logged instruction to Morrow. Without his direct order, Operation Exodus would have to abort.

The hatch to the passenger module was jammed by a buckling of the frame. He left by the command-cabin emergency chute and came down ankle deep in warm sand. Bergman had opened the passenger-module service hatch and was framed in the gap. Behind him, Helena Russell, silver suit streaked with carbon, was repacking a medical bag.

There was no need to enquire about Jansen. Nobody could be alive in the crumpled rear section, where the jammed car had burned to a shell and the cladding of the Eagle was sending up a shimmer of heat haze. Helena spoke over Bergman's shoulder. "I got to him, John. But he was already dead."

Koenig nodded and turned away. From every angle, there was a black, uniformed figure walking forward, closing the circle. Alan Carter dropped through the chute, laser in hand. Koenig said sharply, "Put it away, Captain. I'll try one more time. We're here for a long stay. It's either communicate or die."

To leave no area of doubt about his humanity, Koenig ran down the seals of his space suit and peeled it off. He made a nice mime of unbuckling his equipment belt, with the laser in its clip, and dropped it to the sand. He walked away from the Eagle, straight backed and head tall, looking neither right nor left and aiming for a burly character, with a green sash from shoulder to hip, who seemed to be the top hand in the enterprise.

From ten metres off, he could read a single word, in the local variant of Times Bold, on the leader's sash of office. It meant nothing. Unless it was his name. "Spadec." There was a brief count when Koenig reckoned he would never find the answer. Half a dozen handguns came into aim on the centre of his chest. Nerves crawling in expectation of the blast that would leave an open hatch for his Ka, the Alphan said, "Spadec, my name is John Koenig. We come in peace, but we were forced to defend ourselves."

The leader halted and raised his right hand. The

handguns stayed at the aim, but some of the tension drained away. They had been told to wait.

Koenig's surprise at finding himself still drawing breath into an airtight frame was compounded as the man spoke. He used a combination of speech tones which were an ultimate refinement of speech concepts, so that although the elements were strange, the meaning was clear. It was a skeleton key to unlock communication's door. He said, "I am not Spadec. Spadec is the controlling council of our city. I am Mestor, senior counsellor for security. Who are you?"

The information had been vibrating about the planet for some time and Koenig had to clamp down on mounting frustration to keep his voice steady and factual. "We have tried to communicate. We are from Moonbase Alpha. Our moon was blasted from orbit round its parent planet of Earth. We are seeking a place to live."

Mestor had a high colour and the stand-up neck of his black tunic was a tight fit on his thick neck. His eyes had a blank, fanatical look, as though he only listened closely to himself. He said, "You have killed many of my people. You will stand trial. Spadec will decide what is to be done with you. Tell your companions to surrender their weapons."

The three Alphans had moved slowly and were five paces behind Koenig. Alan Carter's laser was ready for a snap shot at Mestor. There was no doubt, he was likely to be first to fall in any shoot out. But all round the circle, there were handguns lined up on the Alphans. They would all die in the first exchange.

Koenig stalled. "Why did you attack us?"

"Only a fool would wait until an adversary had the advantage over him." Mestor raised his voice and went on. "I will clap my hands five times. At the fifth, my men will fire."

There was no way round it. Mestor could be bluffing, but the smoking car, embedded in Eagle Seven's tail, was proof that these people held their own life cheap. Koenig called out, "Stalemate, Alan. We have nothing

to lose by showing a friendly spirit. Neutralise the
charges and drop your laser."

To Mestor, he said, "Perhaps your council will understand us better. What is the name of this planet?"

"It is Megaron."

"And the city?"

"Caster."

"Are there many such cities? We have seen huge
cities, but deserted. Caster is the first to show any sign
of life."

Mestor was staring over Koenig's shoulder at Helena
Russell. Following Koenig's lead, she had shrugged out
of her space gear and was revealed as the only female
on the set. Carter's suggestion, that charm might out-
weigh diplomacy, suffered a knock. Although the
Megaronian kept his eyes on Helena's elegant figure,
he still spoke to Koenig and the content was no better.
"You ask too many questions. *We* will ask questions.
You are lucky that I do not order summary execution.
You will be taken to my headquarters and interrogated,
so that Spadec will have all the facts."

Reluctantly, he looked away from Helena and made
a mimed signal which would have pleased a choreog-
rapher. It embraced the Alphan group, brought in
selected members of his own party and gave an indica-
tion of the way they were to go. As the speech tones
were an amazing shorthand, for the very essence of
the spoken word, this was, in the same way, a streamlined version of a formal gestural code. Eight men ran
forward from the circle and fell in, two to each Alphan. Nobody seemed to have the slightest curiosity
about Eagle Seven. Mestor swung on his heel and strode
away.

Koenig looked at his time disk. There was less than
one hour to go before Operation Exodus ran into the
sand. He spoke to the man at his left hand. "Do you
have a communication system that I could use to speak
to my people?"

There was no answer. The man had understood, but
the eyes that were turned to look at him had a blank,

empty look. The Megaronian was not interested. He had heard Mestor close the link and it would stay closed. He shrugged and looked away. They reached the hatch of a hover car and Koenig waited, thinking all the Alphans would stay together. But each one, with his escorts, was being led to a different car. There was a little more nonverbal communication. The right-hand marker prodded Koenig with a stiff finger and nodded for him to climb aboard.

Somebody should have warned him about protocol. It was one thing to accept the logic of an untenable situation and go for a dialogue with the authorities, but there was nothing in the small print about being dug in the ribs by a zombie on the way. Koenig hardly moved. He seemed to turn halfway, as though checking out what the man wanted. But his left fist travelled explosively into the guard's diaphragm. The Megaronian buckled forward, leading with his chin and the Alphan could pick his spot for a right cross to the side of the jaw.

It was all very quick and the guard was still waiting for mechanical laws to sort out which way he should fall, as Koenig said, "Tell him not to do that. This gestural dance is a fine thing in its place, but, as commander of Moonbase Alpha, I expect the same courtesy that you would give to your own chief citizen."

It was as well he had spoken and taken the heat out of the situation. The remaining guard listened, as though mesmerised by a talking dog, and eased his finger off of the firing stud of his handgun, where it had already taken first pressure. There was still a brief count when action hung in the balance and Koenig could feel his nerves tense; but he forced himself to move on, swinging through the open hatch into the tender.

There was a pilot, who had remained at his post, and a gunner, standing with his head in a transparent dome that swivelled in concert with the revolving platform he was on. Elbows on a twist-grip firing bar, he watched Koenig come aboard. He was the first one the Alphan had seen who looked genuinely pleased about something.

The guard at the hatch said, "Myndon, help me to lift Gadarn in."

"Is it necessary? Would it not be better to leave him to be found by the Outfarers."

"You take a chance saying that in front of me and the boy. Suppose one of us should tell him, eh? Where would you be then? Come on, move yourself."

Some of the satisfaction drained out of Myndon's face. He still counted the sight of Gadarn going down, like some log, as a precious addition to memory's holographic web; but he saw the wisdom of keeping it a private pleasure. Gadarn was section leader of ten craft and the most notorious bastard in the flight. The stranger had made a bad enemy. Together, the two Megaronians hauled the man aboard. The pilot, a fresh-faced youngster with a golden bird sticker on the left breast pocket of his black tunic, found a round leatherette cushion and stuck it under Gadarn's head.

There was a ping on orchestral A from the instrumentation and the pilot nipped smartly back to his cockpit. The air cars rose like disturbed flies from the sand dunes and streamed in line astern for Caster. Unlike the empty cities they had seen, this one was horizontally planned in its main features. It lay like a cartwheel on a neck of land, that was bounded by open sea to the north and by wide, sandy estuaries to the east and west. There was a broad, surface road round the perimeter and four evenly spaced diameters ran like spokes, dividing the area into eight sectors and one large, circular, central zone, which seemed to be laid out as a public park. There were no tall buildings. Mostly, two storeys had been reckoned as enough. But in the centre, one or two long blocks ran to four floors. It was to the rear of one of these that the long line of air cars directed itself and they peeled off the stick in threes, to drop onto numbered spaces in the parking lot.

Five circled the building, asking for permission to

land. Then they dropped in a close laager on the flat
roof. Gadarn was stirring on his squab and came to full
flower as the car flexed gently on its jacks. He was still
a confused man, but he remembered enough of the
action to know where blame should lie. He hauled
himself to his feet, gripping the handrail so that his
knuckles showed white. He fairly spat out: "You will
pay, Alphan. Be sure of that. You will pay in full
and with something over for my own pleasure."

The pilot said, "The Alphans are to be taken to the
pound to await interrogation. Spadec instruction—
fifty stroke two one four." It was a timely interruption.
Gadarn seemed to be working towards an interim divi-
dend on the account. His eyes, which had been fixed
on Koenig in a malevolent glare, shifted over to Myndon, still at his gunnery post. "The hatch, Gunner;
take this pig out. If he makes any show of resistance,
shoot him in the knees. Even a pig from outer space
will have no vital organ in his kneecaps."

To Koenig, he said, "Outer space my ass. You are
mutants from Hyria. Spadec will sort you out, and
when interrogation is over, I shall add my voice to the
sentencing ceremony."

The city pound was a variant of the deep dungeon
with the hole in the roof that had figured in the history
of Earth Planet. But there were no rats and instead of
a knotted rope, an elevator dropped them down an
open slot in the rock wall. The Alphans had been conducted to ground level, inside the building, down a
wide, central stairway that served all floors. Then they
were dispatched, two at a time, for the last leg of the
journey, into a circular pit that was all of fifty metres
from its white-tiled floor to the distant roof.

All round the circle, the solid rock had been cut out
into narrow, open cells. Each had a slab and a stone
pillow with a hollow for the head. At this time, all cells
were open for inspection, but metal grilles running on
a track could be slid across to pen the prisoner inside.
At mid-points of the circle, two larger cells served as
washrooms. In the middle of the floor there was a

metal pillar with a crosspiece and a selection of clips
to cater to a wide range of ankle and wrist sizes.

Helena Russell said, "They *listen,* but they don't
hear. You might as well save your breath. It's like
trying to talk to patients in a geriatric ward. You think
you've got an idea across, they nod and look as though
they've understood; then the next thing they say shows
that it wasn't so at all. They're on a different wavelength. Certainly, they don't understand about the
Moon. There's just no curiosity about space at all.
There was one in the car who went on about Hyria.
Anything bad was likely to come from Hyria."

Bergman said, "There's something wrong. Something
difficult to put a finger on. There's a lack of spontane-
ous reaction. As if they were under mild sedation."

"That's part of it." Helena Russell was suddenly
sure of the clinical picture. "Low-level hallucinogens.
Used in some ESP research. Makes the subjects more
sensitive to the power of mind acting at a distance."

Alan Carter had been prowling round the cave, only
partly listening to the scientific seminar. For his money,
it was all one. They were down in a hole with no way
of getting out and no viable Eagle to get back to, even
if they did. He said, "I suppose we all realise what
this means to Operation Exodus? It won't be long now
before Paul has to pull the plug. . . ." He stopped.
There was another angle and it was only now in the
quiet vault that his mind had gotten around to it.

Bergman finished it for him. "Which leaves us,
whether we like it or not, to live out our ration of
time on Megaron."

There was something else and all four were stock
still. It was nothing surprising, that the idea should be
in every head. But the form of words used to express
it might have been different for each one. In the
event, Carter could have said, "You took the very
words out of my mouth, Professor."

Koenig, a verbaliser, who tended to see the words
he spoke as a running script in his mind's eye, had
seen the sentence in full before Bergman had spoken

the first two words. Helena Russell's thought patterns were more of colour and shape, but she heard it as though Bergman had been interpreting something from inside the shell of her head. It was uncanny. She said slowly, "Conditions must be specially suited to ESP. Or they *make* them so. It would explain how they act together so well."

Koenig said, "If that's true, and I'm not saying it couldn't be, you'd think they would know the truth without all this aggro. They should know we meant no harm."

Bergman said, "They're on the defensive against people from Hyria. They believe we could be from there. So far we've tangled with the military. Maybe we'll get more sense out of the civilian administration. Or this Spadec, whoever he is."

"Not *he,* but *it.*"

The voice was low, with an urgent, sweet timbre. It came from the opening of a cell, which Carter had not reached on his prowling check. Its owner was on the small side, being about a metre and a half in her foam-soled sneakers. Soma type was fractionally towards the elegant end on the scale running from thin to fat. It was easy to make judgements, since the white sneakers and an electrum bracelet were all she stood up in. Dark hair brushed silkily on her shoulders. Eyes were large, golden brown and very bright. Skin was unifomly tanned a pale brown, except for a crisscross of livid streaks in slanting stripes from left hip to right shoulder.

It had cost her an effort to get on her feet and join the seminar. She put a hand to her head, as though a wave of vertigo had put a surge on her clock and Carter, with reaction times tried and tested in a demanding service, was off the mark at a srping. He caught her as she fell and held her across his arms.

Some powerful instinct of caution cleared her head. Arm hooked round his neck, she hauled herself up to take a good look at the Alphan. Brown eyes stared into blue ones. Carter could see that he had been wrong in supposing that her eyes were one colour over-all. There were small chips of paler gold in the mix. They were as remarkable as anything he had seen on the Moon's odyssey. Like the Egyptian symbol for a million, he was an astonished man. For her part, the girl sighed deeply and relaxed. It was a vote of confidence that touched his heart.

Helena said, "You can't stand there holding her forever, Alan. Put her down and I'll have a look."

Carter went forward into the cell and lowered her gently to the stone slab. He zipped off his tunic top and manoeuvred it underneath and round her. He was still in a state of visual shock and Helena had to move him aside. "It's a girl. Anybody would think you'd never seen one."

An honest man, he said, "I've never seen one with eyes like this one. She must be one of their own people. What's she doing down here?"

"Go away and give me a chance to find out."

In her own medicentre, Helena Russell would have had it sorted out in the minutes it would take to fix a couple of sensors. Working from first principles, with no medical gear, it took longer and it was not easy to be definite. When she joined the others, she said, "As far as I can tell, there's nothing much wrong. I'd say she's suffered a lot of pain. But what's causing this swoon bit has more to do with food. I'd say she's not been eating or drinking for a few days. She needs water at least or she'll be getting properly dehydrated."

Carter had gone to stand by the sick bed and was on hand for a second go of communication. The eyes opened slowly, focussed on his chest and then looked at the stand-up collar of his tunic, which was nearer home. Putting two and two together with quick data analysis, the girl said, "You are being kind to me. Who are you?"

"Carter, Alan Carter. It's a long story. We came from space, trying to make contact with your people. They would not listen."

"I am Rhoda. They are not my people. At least, they are and they are not."

The others had crowded in to hear what was being said. Helena knelt down. "Why are they starving you?"

"They are not. It is I who will not eat their food. We know there is a drug added to the food or the water. We do not know which, so I will take neither."

"Why is that?"

"Why? . . ." Rhoda was having to make an effort to concentrate. "Why? . . . It would make me like them. I would not be able to resist the orders from Spadec. They beat me, but I would not eat. They can kill me, but I will not eat."

Koenig said, "We have seen the word Spadec on the cars and on the guards' armbands. Now you are using it. What does it mean?"

"It is a long story, as Alan says, but it stands for Social, Political and Defence Executive Committee. That is the body which governs the city; but we believe it should now signify something different. . . ."

Eyes closed again. Long black lashes lay in even arcs on smooth skin. Carter said, "We shouldn't push her. She's had a bad time."

Rhoda was in a highly sensitive state, having been needled by pain and hunger and apprehension about whether she had finally gotten to the end of her personal saga. Added to the forces swilling about, which were conducive to ESP, it made her aware of what was going on in Carter's head. *Noblesse oblige.* Such stunned approval deserved encouragement. She opened her eyes again, looked directly at him and managed a luminous smile, which was a kind of holding operation. Carter got a message as if on the Eagle Command net. "I read you, Captain. Sitrep unfavourable for immediate response. Your attitude appreciated. I hope there will be an opportunity for depth investigation. Reluctantly, out. . . ."

She was away again and he was left to debate whether or not he had invented it all for himself or

whether indeed there had been any participation by
Rhoda.

They had been so involved with this first rational
contact with a Megaronian that the elevator cage hit
its stop at the bottom of the shaft before anyone had
noticed that it was even on the way. A harsh, familiar
voice said, "Earthmen—if what you claim is true. Here
is food. Tomorrow, you will be interrogated by the
council."

It was Mestor in person, sharing the cage with two
guards and a food trolley stacked with platters and
covered dishes. Koenig's quick assessment of the odds
was noticed. Mestor pointed to the roof. Where the
elevator trunk pierced the floor above, there was a
gantry, clewed to the rock wall. On it, a couple of
guards were leaned over the handrail, watching the
scene below. If prisoners attacked the warders, there
was a back-up force that could not be reached.

Mestor said, "Relax, Commander. You are not going anywhere or doing anything which does not have
our approval. You might as well cooperate with me,
so that I can arrive at the truth. Your story of a wandering moon will not do. Bring out that fool girl, Nergal. These new guests will see how we treat those who
are obstinate."

Carter had remained inside the cell, leaning on the
wall and watching the slow rise and fall of his jacket
as Rhoda breathed in and out. Nergal brushed past
him and leaned over the cot. He had slapped left and
right to get a little attention from the sleeper, before
the Alphan fully realised what was going on. Rhoda's
small cry, as she was jerked back into the here and
now, dropped his relays and moved him into action.

Rhoda saw Nergal's face directly overhead, then
it was plucked away. Carter had him by the collar of
his tunic and his crotch and swung him in an arc that
thumped his head into the rear wall. Black night filled
Nergal's eyes and he had no further interest as Carter
continued the turn and pitched him out through the
open door.

It highlighted a weakness in the security system. A guard on the high gantry loosed off a shot and a glowing energy ball cracked into the stone lintel, five centimetres from Carter's head.

Thoroughly roused, Rhoda was sitting up with red marks on her skin where Nergal had struck. She said, "You shouldn't have done that. They can't do much more to me, but now they'll start on you."

"What do they want you to tell them?"

"Nothing that they don't already know or couldn't nearly guess."

A further volley sounded from outside. Koenig, Bergman and Helena were on the far side of the circle. The cage was halfway down on a second trip with reinforcements. The men above were making it clear that if the Alphans moved from where they were, they would be shot.

Carter was still seeking information. "But if there's no secret about all this, why get yourself beaten? Are you just plain obstinate?"

Rhoda said in her husky, vibrant voice, that carried absolute conviction, "It's a matter of principle. They have no right to treat me like this. If I give in, they'll think everybody is like *them*. It isn't true. There are still real people in the world."

"Where?"

"The Outfarers. We reject this artificial way of life."

Mestor had got his troops lined up. He said nastily, "Come out of there, Earthman, or both you and that pig of a girl will die."

There was a pause to a count of three and he went on with an uncanny interpretation of what had been going on in Carter's head. "There is nothing more you can do. You are right, you were too hasty. You should have taken Nergal's gun. But even then, it would only have postponed the inevitable."

Carter stroked Rhoda's hair, gave the top of her head a pat and walked steadily for the door. A guard fell in on either side and Mestor said, "Tie him to the post."

It took a little time. Carter judged rightly that nobody had a clear enough view to be sure of hitting him. He had the satisfaction of sending another guard to join Nergal in his cloud of unknowing, before he was hauled by main force to the post and clipped on by ankles and wrists.

Mestor had produced a metre-long, flexible rod and made it whistle in the air. Following a hunch, or using ESP, he had judged that Koenig and Bergman would be more concerned with the woman's safety than their own. He had one guard aiming at point-blank range for Helena's head. He said, "I have no interest in whether she lives or dies, but she will surely die if you interfere."

The rod cracked explosively into Carter's chest to make a period.

Koenig said bitterly, "You are proving that you are barbarians on this planet of Megaron. Where is the civilisation that built the cities we have seen?"

Mestor picked his spot and struck again. He said, "You are speaking of the land of Hyria, and their vaunted civilisation came near to destroying life forever on Megaron. The ultimate civilisation is here in Caster, where all the people are satisfied with the life they have."

He was about to strike again, when Rhoda's voice spoke from the cell door. "That is a lie, Mestor, and you know it. The people have no will of their own to know whether they are satisfied or not. I will make a bargain with you. Do not punish the stranger and I will answer some of your questions."

Carter had beads of sweat standing on his forehead and there was a trickle of blood on his chin from a convulsive bite at his lower lip. Keeping his voice level, he said, "Don't sell out on my account, Rhoda. We all have principles."

Mestor considered the rod and seemed to be waiting for the decision to come from elsewhere. Finally, he said, "Very well. There is all the time in the world. None of you are going anywhere. Tomorrow you will be questioned directly by the Council. Keep to your bargain and your punishment may be no more than a year in the rehabilitation centre. I will leave you to think about it. This madman can stay where he is."

Mestor and his guards made an orderly withdrawal, taking no chances.

Rhoda, kept on her feet by her new interest, walked slowly across to the victim in the pillory and leaned on him with her hands on his shoulders. Failing medicare, it was as soft and healing a pad as anybody could have put on the spot.

Helena Russell, finding her occupation gone, turned her attention to the food trolley. There was fruit, a container of some cereal product that could be an oat porridge, a tall stoppered jug, full of a rose-pink liquid, and some round, brown biscuits like teething rusks. Koenig asked, "What about it, Helena? Can you make any judgement? Rhoda seems quite sure they put in an additive."

"I'd need lab facilities to be sure. We could take a chance on probabilities. It would be easiest to fix the drink. Least easy to fix the fruit."

Bergman said, "In the situation we find ourselves, we have to ask whether it matters. As far as I can see, we have nothing to conceal. The drug, if it exists, seems to be designed to make the mind more open to suggestion. It's probably cumulative. Taken over a decade, it might leave you mindless as a brush. But in the short term, you have to weigh it against going without food. For that matter, fasting is hallucinatory. There's not much difference in mental condition between a fasting saint and some self-indulgent yobo on a trip."

Koenig said, "You can't believe that, Victor. There's all the difference in the world."

"There's a difference in what they make of it, but some of the electrochemical changes in the brain are very similar."

Carter said, "I'll settle for a drink and take my chance on having a bad trip."

Koenig looked at his time disk. He said, "Paul will be making a last call."

It was true, within a second. Even as he finished speaking, Paul Morrow's voice was going out from the leading Eagle. "Eagle Fleet Command calling Eagle Seven. Do you read me? Come in, Eagle Seven."

There was no answer. The passenger module of the Eagle had been set up as executive command post for the mission. He looked at Sandra and at Kano. There was no comfort and no getting around the decision already on the file. He said, heavily, "That's it, then. We abort the mission. Get the signal out, Sandra. It's a straight run to Moonbase Alpha."

"What about the commander?"

"There's been nothing from Eagle Seven since they went close in. They would signal if they could, you can be sure of that."

"So you believe they are dead?"

"I believe they are unable to signal."

"So they could be alive and we are proposing to leave them?"

"An Eagle could not reach the planet, search for them, find them and still get back to Moonbase Alpha, because of the unique trajectory the Moon has taken in this case."

"I know that."

"But you want to make it clear for the record that you don't like any part of it?"

Sandra Benes could not see through the direct-vision port. Her eyes were full of tears, which she made no effort to wipe away. But her voice was rock steady as she called, "Eagle Fleet Command to all Eagles. There is no signal from Eagle Seven. It has to be assumed that the ship is lost. Operation Exodus is cancelled. The Eagle Fleet will return to Moonbase Alpha. Stand by for course data. . . ."

The silvery Eagles, strung like a bead chain over the star map, swung in an arc behind the Eagle leader. There was no one on Megaron with the skill or interest to watch them go. Time was, when interceptor craft from Hyria would have been out already to check on the visitors, but no longer. The great cities were dead. Here and there, smaller enclaves like Caster had picked up the guttering torch and were looking about them. But, for the most part, there was nothing spare to go for outreach. They were content to snap up the unconsidered trifles of the golden ages and keep their eyes down.

Skies darkened over the city. Lights brightened in the streets. Carter fidgeted in his pillory. Rhoda lay on his coat, close to his feet. Helena Russell raised her head from Koenig's arm and listened in the semidarkness. It was not easy to identify, but there was a thump and a scrabble and a vibration. If it had any point of origin, it seemed to be coming from under the floor.

CHAPTER THREE

Koenig swung himself out of the narrow bunk and padded to the opening of the cell. There was one small ceiling port still lit, close to the observation gantry. The lumen count at floor level was low enough to take out colour and leave the set in shades of grey. Carter lifted his head. He had found the pillory a shrewd device for making a man think of personal priorities. There was no real sleep to be had. He reckoned anyone held in it for a week would be all set to sign a paper giving his freehold to the establishment. There had been no way to beat the snap locks. He was stuck with his post of honour until the morning.

Koenig said sympathetically, "How does it go?"

"I'll live."

"Did you hear anything?"

"Like what, for instance?"

"Helena thought there was something going on below decks."

Rhoda stirred and sat up, a pale alabaster figure in the dim light. "What is it? Are you all right, Alan? I am so sorry you are there. Is there anything I can do for you?"

"You can be quiet and listen."

"What am I supposed to be listening for?"

"Nobody knows until we hear it."

"I will try."

"Do that."

"I am doing it now."

If he had been free to do it, Carter would have thumped his forehead with the flat of his hand. What Rhoda would be like when full of sap and vigour was a question to ponder on. Even in her reduced state, she gave off zeal like some dynamo.

The noise was repeated and sounded nearer. Koenig flattened his ear to the deck and the detail was easier to sort out. Some kind of digging device was being used. A shaft was being driven upwards towards the floor they were on.

Rhoda copied the technique. She had allowed herself to be persuaded to eat a piece of fruit and drink a few cc.'s of the pink liquor. She was still feeling frail and in a highly suggestible state, but covered more ground than Koenig like an eager rabbit. It was she who stopped with an emotional quiver and said, "Here it is. Just underneath here. I can hear it."

Koenig joined her. She was right. From this angle, there was the click and scrape of tools working close to the surface.

Helena Russell had been busy waking Bergman. Both joined the party. She reckoned she came in the nick of time, or Koenig would have been giving Rhoda's eloquent seat a congratulatory pat. Rhoda sat back on her heels in a taut, unself-conscious pose that made Carter rattle his chains for a little attention.

"So you found it? What do you have, for God's sake?"

Rhoda straightened too quickly and was reeling from sudden vertigo as she crossed the floor to tell him. Supporting herself with one hand on his chest and using the other for dramatic gestures, she said, "It will be my friends. My uncle, Karl, is elected leader of the Outfarers for this year. I know he will have been thinking very hard about how to release me. They have tunnelled under the city."

Bergman said, "How long have you been here?"

"Oh, four, perhaps five days."

"How far away is the Outfarers' camp?"

"Perhaps thirty kilometres."

"Nobody can dig that sort of tunnel in four days."

"That is true." She turned confidentially to Alan Carter. "That old brainy-looking friend of yours is right, Alan. How do you explain it?"

There was no time to work on it. Koenig grabbed for Helena and threw her clear as a ragged hole opened at her feet and a small cloud of grey dust ballooned around them. There was a pause, a definitive thump, as a last loose hunk of rubble broke away and dropped down the shaft and then a longer silence. Helena thought soberly that if the tunnellers were anywhere near as impulsive as Rhoda, they would be lying shattered underneath the rockfall.

The dust thinned and settled and the head of a ladder was revealed poking a handsbreadth over floor level. All except Carter were standing round it in a ring to see the dome of a miner's helmet appear, followed by broad, powerful shoulders and a fist holding a heavy machine pistol.

Rhoda was on hands and knees to check him in. She said, "Karl! I knew you'd find me."

Twisting her head to speak over her shoulder and bring Carter into the group, she called, "Alan! This is Karl. Now you will be all right."

Karl heaved himself out of the hole. Wherever Rhoda was, there was likely to be an animated scene, but there was clearly more going on than he expected. He was a short, powerfully built man with a close-trimmed, greying beard and deep-set eyes. His voice had some of Rhoda's husky vibration in it as he said, "Who are these people, Rhoda?"

"You won't believe it, Karl."

"Try me."

"They're not from Megaron at all."

Told her way, it was going to take some time. He said hastily, "It will have to wait. We should get out of here. The question is whether or not they are to come with us."

"Of course they come with us. They helped me.

And Alan over there got himself whipped on my account."

"Go down. I will see to it. Send up Lampon and Eris."

Rhoda went back to Carter, picked his tunic from the deck and draped it over her shoulders. A quick pressure and she was away again and the prison floor seemed quieter and less full of people. Koenig said, "We cannot leave without Captain Carter."

Karl was already assembling a power tool that worked from a hand pumped generator. He said, "We were not sure whether Rhoda would be free to move or whether there would be restraints. This will cut most metals."

Bergman said, "A vibrator?"

"The same. You know of this principle?"

Lampon and Eris came through the hatch, dressed like Karl in round miner's helmets and a semimilitary rig of pants and battle-dress top in olive drab.

Lampon leaned on the nearest wall and fixed his eyes on the distant gantry, his machine pistol aimed at the hatch. Eris joined his leader and they made a quick, methodical job of shearing away Carter's clips. Karl said, "Go down. We will bring him. Go down. You will find the others at the first intersection."

There was nothing to wait for. In a manner of speaking, they had come naked into this world and were leaving it without having gathered any possessions. Last to go, Koenig saw Carter move stiffly from his post.

The shaft was hardly two metres deep. It had been broken through from the roof of a massive, brick-lined culvert. There was a support file at the bottom of the ladder to wave him on after the column. In the bottom of the culvert, there was a black cable with a diameter of at least a metre and a half, carried on saddles spaced every ten paces. Lights ahead showed where the rest of the party were waiting. He balance-walked along the top of the cable. Bergman met him. "That's a fantastic power cable, John. I'd say it was a relic from an older city. But where does it come from and, for that matter, where does it go?"

The intersection was made by another culvert cutting across at right angles. Four more men, all heavily armed, were waiting for the signal to move on. It soon came. Karl was clearly not one to hang about. The ladder had been broken down into three sections and each of the final assault group had a piece when they appeared along the cable.

Karl made no stop, turned left into the intersection, which was wider, but not as high as the culvert, and picked his way over a ribbed floor littered with loose cables and the maintenance covers of lighting ports.

Fifty metres on, two men were waiting at an open trap and the ladder was assembled again for a drop into a large tunnel, walled with white ceramic tiles in metre-square sections and with a pale-green ribbed floor, a centimetre deep in grey dust like the finest talcum powder. When all were assembled and the hatch shut, there were enough lamps on the set to give fair light for fifty metres all round. As they moved off, the fine dust rose thigh deep in a swirling cloud. Rhoda had found Alan Carter and was holding his hand. After all the aggro, it was a surrealist-type sequence, like finding a drawing room at the bottom of a lake.

Koenig stopped thinking. It could be as Rhoda had said, that the food was doped. His mind was open and accepting. If Karl had led them in a circle and back up the shaft into the prison, he would have gone on putting one foot after the other. Beside him, Helena Russell was in a similar state. His left hand was comfortably chocked on her hip. He could feel the supple movement, proving that they were in fact walking, but they could have been drifting in a cloud.

There was no sense of time or distance gone, but there was a change. Karl had opened a service panel in the right-hand wall. There was a confusing scramble through a number of ducts and conduits and another drop using the ladder. This time they came out into a

tunnel which showed signs of more recent use. The
roof had a deep box-section slot which was the housing
for a continuous metal strip. Waiting for the party was
a low, toast-rack trolley with seats for fifty. It had
very small wheels and only centimetres of ground
clearance. Duplicate control consoles were set at either
end and in the middle, a spring-loaded contact bar
was swung up like a mast to within a few centimetres
of the metal strip.

The embussing operation took only seconds and
Karl was thumping the engineer on his tin hat for him
to take it away.

The power scoop clunked home for a full due. A
motor began to hum and the trolley was away in a
smooth surge. Once the operation was successful, Karl
seemed to have forgotten about the brands plucked
from the burning. He sat behind his driver, hands in
pockets, hunched down in his coat and looking dead
ahead.

The air was fresh, colder, with a damp chill about
it. Helena shivered. This molelike tunnelling and the
whole bit since Eagle Seven had dived low over Caster
was a far cry from what they had expected of Megaron. She could see Koenig's profile, set and hard, as
he stared ahead. It was worse for him. Knowing the
way his mind worked, she knew he would be blaming
himself for the decision that had robbed Alpha of four
senior executives and landed that same quartette on
a dogs' island.

She twisted in her seat to look up the car. All the
light from the lamps was forward and it was not easy
to make out who was in the rumble. But there were
two without hats. Rhoda never missed a trick. There
was one Alphan, at least, who would have a hard row
to hoe, if he wanted to find an unfilled minute to cata-
logue his regrets.

On her other side, Victor Bergman was still batting,
watching the gear and changing features of the underground system. He felt her eyes on him and managed
a wry smile.

"How do you feel, Victor?"

"Better all the time. Rhoda was right. There was an additive in that food. Wearing off now, but for people eating it regularly, there'd be a compulsion to accept anything that was going on without opposition."

"When you think about it, that's the ultimate in social engineering. Contentment all round."

"But who decides where the level is that's acceptable?"

"Does it matter?"

Bergman looked closely at her. "That's a more cynical remark than I ever expected to hear from you, Helena."

"A position for argument only."

"I'm glad to hear it."

The character of the tunnel changed. It opened out in height and width. Massive cross-ribs ran from side to side and the power feed was carried on hanging pylons. The note of the motor dropped to a growl and they climbed a long, easy incline with a sudden change overhead, as they ran into an open cutting crossed by flyovers.

It was a warm, Mediterranean-type night, with stars in unfamiliar constellations. Koenig could imagine his Eagle fleet coming into a landfall on such a night. Instead, his people were beating back to the silent cinder heap that had carried them across the galaxy. It was a lot to accept.

The right-hand wall of the cutting peeled away and they were running on a corniche with open sea reflecting the myriad stars and one feature that was clearly a novelty to Karl and his party. Earth's moon was racing across the night sky of Megaron for a one-off performance.

They rounded a bluff, bore inland for a kilometre and the open trolley slowed to a stop in what had been the basement of some immense building. The squat piers that supported the roof were designed to bear a tremendous load; but, in fact, the glimpse they had of the structure, before they went under it, showed that there was only one intact floor, and above that, a gaunt tangle of twisted girder work and fallen masonry, rearing its grotesque bulk against the sky, like a man-made Eiger.

Karl said, "Come," and led the way up a broad ramp which gave access to the ground floor. They im-merged into a vast lobby with subdued lighting that had no identifiable source.

Rhoda said, "This is where the Outfarers live. There is plenty of room. We hardly use a tenth of the space. If you are accepted, you will be given an apart-ment and put on the schedules for whatever kind of work you can do. That will be easy for you, Helena, being a doctor. There's a whole clinic, but no really professional staff. Then there's the technical service and the defence corps." She gave Alan Carter a con-fidential pat. "A niche for everybody, you might say."

Koenig was talking to Karl. "Will there be reprisals? They will know where to look."

"So far we have had very little trouble from Caster. They don't like to send their people much beyond a ten-kilometre zone round the city. Outside that limit, the mental control field is too weak to be fully effec-tive. What we get, we can deal with. You will under-stand, when I show you our organisation. But first, there will have to be a meeting. You will have to be accepted by all the people." •

"That sounds like democracy in action."

"The community is still small enough to make de-mocracy a workable system. Tonight, I will find you accommodation close to my quarters. Come this way."

In its heyday, the first floor of the ziggurat had been given over to public rooms and admin spreads. To bring in a domestic scale, divisons had been run up to make apartments. Even so, they had tended to give themselves plenty of elbow room. Karl's pad had a lounge area twenty-metres square with one wall as a continuous observation window, overlooking the sea.

As they trekked through it, a small, dark woman, in a flame caftan, jacked herself out of a club chair and almost ran to meet them. Rhoda had stayed with the party to see them settled and there was enough family likeness to make no surprise when she said, "Mother. You waited up for me! Alan, this is my mother, Gelanor."

In point of fact, Gelanor's eyes had been on Karl, and the open pleasure she was clocking up showed her concern for his safe return. In appearance, she was a mature version of Rhoda, with slightly buck teeth that kept her full lips in a permanent, good-natured smile. Reminded of nature's call, and with hardly less delight, she changed course and converged on her daughter.

"Rhoda, my pet! Karl got you out. I knew he would. I said to myself, 'If anybody can free Rhoda from that vile place, it will be Karl.' And I was right, wasn't I? How do you feel, my precious? What did they do to you, then? Why are you wearing that bizarre jacket? That colour is *not* for you. . . ."

Rhoda had made several efforts to break in without success. Cued in by the fashion angle, she slipped off Carter's tunic and Gelanor was silenced. Soberly, she took Rhoda's hand. "Oh, my dear. I *am* sorry. We moved as soon as we could. But there was much to plan. Karl and I were frantic for you. And Melanion—"

"Where *is* my father?"

"On duty in the power centre. You know there is no one else with the knowledge he has of the power circuits. Without power in those old tunnels, nothing could have been done. Where are you taking them, Karl?"

"That spare suite next door."

"Before they go, they must have something to eat and drink. Make them comfortable. It won't take long."

Being home and dry suddenly got to Rhoda. The pressures of the jailbreak had kept her moving. Now, all the weariness of the past days pushed over the threshold. Carter, who was getting to be the Alpha expert in the field, caught her as her knees crumpled, and Gelanor said, almost humbly, "I am the most thoughtless parent. I should have seen she was overstrained. Alan, isn't it? Alan, bring her along. The rest of you make yourselves comfortable. I shall not be long."

The family apartment was another divison of the long room, reaching through an arch hung with a tinkling bead curtain. Following the animated wiggle of her expressive back, Carter disappeared, to an ironic wave from Koenig. Coping with a mother would be breaking new ground for his chief pilot, and it looked as though he had met his Waterloo.

Helena said, "Don't be like that, John. He's enjoying it. She's a very nice girl."

"I can see that."

"So I've noticed. Perhaps you'd rather be doing it yourself?"

There was no immediate answer to that one and he conducted her formally to a deeply cushioned chair. Gelanor was as good as her word. It was likely that she had it all ready for the party's return. She was in again, before the sudden silence had gotten out of hand. Carter, the new household favourite, was carrying a large tray.

There was a tall, white pot of dark liquid, which tasted not unlike hot chocolate when their hostess had handed it around in delicate, ceramic beakers and some freshly baked biscuits stamped out to a heart shape.

Gelanor said, "Now, don't be taciturn, Karl. Tell them about us."

"About Megaron?"

"Don't they know about Megaron?"

"They say they came from another planet. On that moon that appeared."

She appealed to Bergman, since he looked most like a sage. Squatting on her heels, with her flame caftan falling dramatically from the jut of her full breasts, she opened her eyes wide. "Is that *true*? Did you come from there?"

"It is true enough. We were the advance party. We were to signal the rest of our people to follow, if Megaron was fit for occupation. But we were attacked near Caster and the signal was never made. The fleet will have turned back. We have no ship, no choice, but to stay."

Karl said slowly, "Megaron had an advanced civilisation so long ago that the records we have do not tell of its beginning. Caster is a barbaric village compared with what had been. The ruins of the great cities are all that remain of the last great phase. But we know that there have been many civilisations that have risen and flourished and then died. As long as there are a few free survivors like ourselves, the process will start over again. We shall not see it, but there will be a great future yet for Megaron."

Helena said, "We crossed a great continent, which I believe you call Hyria. There was evidence of radiation. Life there would be hazardous for some years yet."

"True. Life *here* is not completely straightforward. We live unnaturally, as you see, amongst the ruins. But a great deal of the farmland is poisoned. We could not feed very many more people than we have at the moment. We use a hydroponic system, and that puts a limit on production."

Koenig, who had been thinking that his Eagle fleet ought to have taken a chance and landed, looked more cheerful. "So the Alphans could not have landed anywhere and started a farming commune?"

"Not at all. By no means. You would all have been dead in a week. Turning up the soil would release nerve gases. We are working very slowly to clear a few hectares on this peninsula."

Bergman asked, "Are there other communities besides Caster?"

"There are some, we believe, but we have no communication. Nor do we want any, until we are stronger. Who knows how they have organised themselves? Caster has gone to one extreme to preserve itself without change. Others might be worse."

Helena Russell said, "How did you get here?"

"Most of us were born here. There has been a small community of Outfarers in this place for several centuries at least. From time to time others have found their way to join us. Equipment and supplies are plentiful. Water from the sea, through a desalination plant. Food from the hydroponic farm. Time is on our side. We can move slowly."

Koenig considered it. In the quiet circle of lamp light, surrounded by the trappings of comfort, it was a viable way of life. But Helena chimed with his thinking when she said, "It is Moonbase Alpha over again and maybe time is not as firmly on your side as you suppose. As I understand it, there is no standing still. Living is struggling and a community either goes forward or regresses."

Karl stood up and took his beaker to the tray. He said, "It is late. I can see we shall have some interesting discussions. Thank you, Gelanor. I will take them to their quarters. We will all meet in the morning."

Except for a small duty group, detailed to keep the eager young busy, and a few oldsters who were relieved of all citizen responsibilities, there was a full set of Outfarers to hear the Alphans present their case. The venue was an actualiser theatre where the long-gone Megaronians of the tower block had watched sophisticated 3-D presentations on a circular stage in the centre of the auditorium.

There was a line of chairs on the platform, four for the Alphans over on the left, five for Karl and his management team. The hoi polloi filled three rows of the front stalls. House lights were dimmed and the platform party were isolated in a shaft of light from a battery of spots on a boom.

Koenig reckoned there could be a couple of hundred out front, and suddenly realised that they were involved in something more than a formality. Karl had introduced the business and was doing a fair job of being a neutral chairman. When he had finished, the floor had been given an open choice. Karl had explained that if the Alphans were accepted, they would be full citizens with a right to negotiate pairing contracts, and that this would involve the acceptance of an alien genetic strain into the Megaronian stock. The consequences could be good or bad, but they would certainly bring change. The strangers had skills to offer, but they would also have ideas which might rock the boat.

Nobody on the platform had anything to add and Karl threw it open to speakers from the floor. Rhoda was first on her feet, identifiable by her voice, which was husky and passionate in support. A more sober, male voice followed, urging a period of trial. This was a very unusual case and they should meet again, when they knew more about the Alphans. Meantime, they could be given temporary status.

The debate went on for a half hour by Koenig's time disk, before one speaker said that it would help him to make up his mind if a spokesman for the Alphans could speak a piece.

Karl turned to the Alphans. "Which of you will speak?"

Koenig stood up and moved forward. There had been some chatter and lack of concentration as some citizens lost interest. The tall, impressive figure of the Alphan made an impact. There was a sudden hush. If they were expecting an appeal, they were heading for disappointment. Koenig had never been one to compromise. He began slowly. "People of Megaron, this is your place. The decision is yours. We can only abide by it. In our long journey, we have seen many peoples. Some patterns of life have seemed incredible to us. Your way is, on the whole, the nearest to our own that we have seen. But I tell you, the difference between all life, anywhere, and the great blank of unknowing in the interstellar spaces is so great, that all life forms fall in one pan of the scale. What is common to intelligent life is more important than any differences. For our part, we believe in the future and we will fight for it. The freedom of the human spirit to work out its own salvation, we take to be an inalienable right. That right is denied in the city. At some point, we would want to try to bring back freedom there. Because, make no mistake, their system is a barbarism and in any long confrontation between barbarism and civilisation, barbarism will win out, unless the civilised people take the initiative. The choice is yours."

Karl was looking grave. He was ready to accept the principles, but as an experienced politician, he wished Koenig had taken a softer line.

There was only one comment from the floor. A woman's voice said, "We have heard enough. Take the vote."

There was an orderly bustle and tellers moved along the rows with collecting boxes. House lights went up and the audience was no longer anonymous. The boxes were brought forward and the contents spilled out on the table in front of the chairman. Karl began to make stacks of ten with red and black draughtsmen. He had twelve stacks of red and nine and a half stacks of black. He said, "The majority are in favour of accepting the Alphans. But it is not a clear majority, which would require two-thirds in favour. I rule, therefore, that the executive will vote having regard to this opinion expressed by the meeting."

On his left he had his brother, Melanion, an older version of himself with a balding head and an unsmiling face. Beyond him was a younger man, who had been watching Carter with a speculative eye. His ID badge said Golgos. On the right was an oldster, Urion, and on the far right, the only woman on the executive, a trim brunette in a green tabard, labelled Hepa.

Karl passed round a closed box with a slot in the lid. All were discreet. It was impossible to see how they voted. When he opened the box and held up the counters, there were two red and two black. He said, "The rules of this assembly are plain. The decision has been put in my hand. Very well. I have to tell you that I judge in the Alphans' favour. They are admitted to citizenship as Outfarers."

There was sporadic applause, which masked, for a few seconds, a noise which had been slowly rising to the threshold of attention. Inside the hall, there was sudden silence, as everybody strained to listen. To those passing a black counter, it was almost a vindication and a judgement. The forces of law and order in Caster had been needled into action and were out to redress the balance. A squadron of air cars was sweeping in over the Outfarers' sanctuary.

In spite of the grandiose label given to it, the defence corps had only twenty citizens in full-time service. There was a fall-back militia force of a hundred men and women with some training in the use of arms; but to mobilise them for any length of time would put the base on a hand-to-mouth footing, which could only be maintained for a few days. In living memory, it had not been needed, and in the sudden emergency, the first reaction was to leave it to the professionals.

There was an orderly scatter to hearth and home. Karl, after a hard look at his brother, swept the voting counters into their box. He said, "Professor, I'd like you to join Melanion. He can show you something of our technical setup. Commander, you and Captain Carter come with me. Doctor Russell can assist at our medical centre, and I only hope her services won't be needed."

Given the sheer size of the complex and the few defenders, Koenig could only suppose there was no military genius in Caster, or the Outfarers would have been overrun before this. The defence corps was already assembled at a supply point and Golgos, a taciturn, bearded type, was handing out machine pistols and a bandolier of clips to every man. There was a shatter of glass as a car stormed along the sea frontage strafing a line of living quarters. But it was more nuisance value than serious attack. There was no

way for a car to land there and get its crew into the
building.

Golgos took half the company and raced off along
the corridor. Karl took the rest and they went at a jog
trot for the ramp that came up from the basement. As
they went, he jerked out, "Only two ways into this
level. Two ramps we can defend."

Carter said, "Can't they get in from above?"

"The cars could not land."

It could be true, but Carter could see a determined
and skillful pilot finding a toehold to drop a com-
mando party. He said no more. They were at the head
of the stairs. The noise of the air cars was plainer.
There was a drumming reverberation as at least one
dived along the track of the runabout service and a
sudden firework shower of explosive charges as it fired
under the basement itself.

Karl's party had flung themselves down in a line at
the top of the ramp and sent a withering volley at
nothing in particular. Training was too strong for Koenig. He snapped out, "Hold your fire," in an authori-
tative command that checked them all.

There was silence. The car appeared briefly, between two distant support piers and then sidled away
out of view. Koenig said, "It isn't an attack. It's reconnaissance. Don't show our positions or our strength.
If and when they're serious, they'll use ground forces
with the cars in support. With your permission, Karl,
I'll take Captain Carter and we'll go take a look."

"Help yourself."

Bent double in the shelter of the continuous, solid
parapet, the Alphans ran down the ramp into the
basement area. They were in a stone jungle with an
endless vista of support piers in every direction. Cover
was no problem. Koenig worked towards the land side,
believing that any serious attempt at mounting an assault would come that way. There was no sign that
any other car had penetrated below the building and it
would need a cool and experienced pilot to take a
machine that way.

There was still a lot of noise overhead as the squadron made its show of force. When they reached the outer edge of the basement, they could see debris showering down. The Outfarers would have a big repair programme ahead. Koenig cautiously left the shelter of the last, squat pier and moved out on a flagged terrace which ran all round the ruined building. A racing scan round the set confirmed his thinking. There were three cars in line astern on this side and they had worked along the frontage. They were rising and turning. Even as he watched, they were joined by three more which had come from round back and had been strafing the seaward-facing rooms.

Carter's shout and the clatter of his pistol had him diving back for cover. A seventh car, no doubt the one which had been nosing in towards the ramp, had suddenly appeared in a murderous rush along the terrace. As it passed, its rear gunner sprayed into the vaults and the curious energy charges flared like star shells as they bounced and ricocheted amongst the columns.

The six were waiting for the seventh to join. When it took its place as flight leader, they were away, arrowing off over the hill in the direction of Caster.

Koenig watched them go, standing out on the terrace. He said, "They know that the Outfarers have no air defences. They know they can do that anytime they like. The question is whether or not they want a final solution. I guess they could wipe out this enclave if they thought it was worth it."

Carter said, "If they don't regard it as a threat, why should they bother? They would lose some men."

"But they don't care too much about that, as we saw ourselves. I wouldn't want to say this too loudly, but it could be that our arrival tips the scale. Rightly or wrongly, they might believe that we disturb the balance of power."

"These Outfarers are no fools. Some thought of that and passed in those black chequers."

"Could be. But what would you say was the standard answer in a situation where a small power is expecting an attack from a larger and more powerful neighbour?"

"Get in first."

"That's the way I see it. We're here. We aim to survive. I don't like it one little bit, but we haven't come all this way to end up as sitting ducks for some black-coated zombies, whatever the glories of their past. Now, Karl is a man open to a reasoned argument. We should talk to him and see what there is in this scrap heap that we could use. Are you with me?"

"All the way, Commander."

CHAPTER FOUR

The more Koenig thought about it, the more he was convinced that there was no other way. On Karl's own submission, there was no place for the Outfarers to go. They were stuck on their neck of land, with only the immediate neighbourhood of the ruin as a place to live. If Caster was set on rooting them out, it was fight or go under.

But there was another idea coming to the bubble in his head. A preemptive strike might buy them time, but it was not the final solution. The real answer would lie in getting a change of heart in Caster itself. As he understood it, there were two elements that kept Spadec in the saddle. The people, by their own choice or not, had gotten used to a diet which included an intake of drugs, so that they questioned nothing. Together with some subliminal suggestion technique, which was on stream, like a constant carrier wave, this was enough for a totally static society. A community could not stand still—it went forward or back. But that was only true if it was free to move. In this situation, there was equilibrium. Forces had been set up to resist change.

Almost all the rooms with an open view had been strafed and there would be months of work before they were back in full use. The Alphans had a temporary suite in the centre area. It had been an information centre. There were study carrels with selector gear so that data from a storage silo was on tap at the flick of a switch. No longer operative. One wall had a stylised diagram of the complex as it had been in its heyday, and Bergman was finding matters of wonder by the minute, as he walked its length while eating his biscuits and cheese simulate.

Rhoda had joined them on the pretext that Helena would need help to open food dispensers and issue the rations. She sat facing Carter, fixing him with a bright eye and eating compulsively to make up for the loss.

Koenig asked her, "What are the people in Caster like? Are they good people or bad?"

"What they did to me and to Alan could not be called good."

"Not just the guards. The ordinary people."

"They are law abiding. They do what Spadec tells them. They are neutral. They are not really *people* at all."

Helena said, "More like puppets?"

"What are puppets."

"Mechanical dolls, operated by strings so that they go through the motions. Children play with them on Earth Planet and make them act out scenes in plays."

"What a good idea. We could do that in the nursery. I'll mention it to Hepa and Gara. But why do you concern yourself about Caster, Commander Koenig?"

"As I see it, the future lies there. The Outfarers can only hang on from one generation to the next. Caster is big enough to be the starting point for a new civilisation on Megaron. What drug will it be, Helena?"

"There are several that would serve. Some variant of what was once used on Earth Planet as a truth drug?"

"Could you work out an antidote?"

"I shouldn't think it would be necessary. All they have to do is to stop taking it."

Victor Bergman was quicker off the mark. He left the information panel and joined them at the table. "Do I read you right, John? Are you thinking of a neutraliser? Another additive that would make the drug ineffective?"

"Something like that."

Bergman mused, "Interesting. Now, if that could be introduced without their knowledge, without alerting Spadec, that would be a move forward. It might start self-criticism. They'd begin to think for themselves."

Helena Russell said, "Thinking by itself is no guarantee that they'd move in the right direction. It could make them worse. You have to remember that there are some psychotic types that can't be trusted to behave rationally unless they're given suppressive drugs."

Rhoda had been watching each speaker and was ready with a telling piece of logic. "But we *know* what happens when the drugs are not used. The Outfarers are Megaronians just like the people of Caster. We don't use them. That's why we're here—to *avoid* using them. You saw all the people at the meeting. You wouldn't say they were *worse* for it."

There was no answer to that one. The assembled Outfarers had looked like any cross section of any human community. They were living vindication of the theory.

Koenig said, "Then it's something to work on. Three steps. Identify the drug. Manufacture a reagent. Introduce it into the supply."

There was a pause. Carter said, "I'm surely glad you didn't say three *easy* steps, Commander. But to break it down, we need samples of the food. Then it's up to Doctor Russell to come up with analysis and production of the antidote. Stage three would be very delicate indeed, since we don't know how and where it gets into the food chain."

There was help from Rhoda. She had listened to Carter with flattering attention, as though to some oracle. When he stopped, she said, "We can start right away. There are samples of the food here already, but we have not succeeded in isolating the drug. Doctor Russell might be able to do that. There is only one place where it can be added to the food chain. All the food products are made up from a protein staple which is processed in the hydroponic farm spread outside Caster. I know the way. But getting inside would be a problem. I do not think the railway would serve us a second time and, indeed, it does not go in that direction, as far as I know."

Bergman went back to his stylised diagram. He called across, "John, what do you make of this?"

To orientate the searcher, there was a blue asterisk which marked the place they were in. The wall was parallel to the outer wall facing the estuary. The tongue of land which held the ruined tower block and Caster itself was faintly shaded in red, the rivers and the sea were pale green. Caster could be seen on the estuary of the second river. There was a land route marked with a miniature model of a toast rack which could be moved along it to a terminus.

The others lined up beside Koenig and Bergman. Rhoda pointed a supple finger at a collection of circles between Caster and the sea. "There it is. That's the farm spread. It must have been there, even when this tower was a town. It could have been one of the supply farms for this very place. You see, Caster is shown there, but it isn't very big. Just a perimeter wall and some living spaces. I expect it was first used to accommodate the people who worked on the farms. Look, you can see other farm spreads marked out. That would be it. It was a *collection* centre."

Carter picked out another feature. "There was a sea route. That looks like a wharf close to the farm." He walked along the panel following a faint dotted line. "It comes all round the point and ends up here, below the tower. It was always the most economical way to shift bulk supplies. You could work an auto freighter on a fixed course. Bring it in at the basement."

Again Rhoda had information. "There's a whole complex down there. I've been there with Melanion. They need to check sometimes. We get power from a tidal race. It's pretty well self-maintaining, but once in a while something clogs the intake. You can get out into the sea in diving gear. There's a swimming pool on this floor and the intake for it comes in that way, through a filter system."

Koenig cleared his mind of the last lingering regrets for Alpha. They were here to stay. The best therapy they could have would be to get down to a piece of work that would put them on load. He said, "Right then, I'll find Karl and get him to take us down there. Meantime, Helena, if you go to work in the lab, you could try to crack this drug. The only thing we can do if we hang about is grow older."

Helena Russell allowed a half-formed thought to pass—the plan that was taking shape gave every chance that those involved in it would not get much older—but she stifled it, loyally. She said, mildly, "If Rhoda would come with me, it might be easier to explain what I'm doing."

Rhoda looked disappointed, but saw the wisdom of it.

At every point, the sheer scale of the ancient enterprise made Earth-type planning look like a child's game in a playpen. But Koenig held fast to the simple truth that all their progress had finally run into the sand. It was all a vindication for Bergman's thesis that small is beautiful and too much reliance on technical progress, as an end in itself, was not what human life should be all about.

Karl took them through Melanion's workshop section to an elevator which dropped them below the basement level into what had been an underground seaport, no less. There was even a broad-beamed freighter, dry-docked in an immense empty basin. Melanion had grudgingly turned on some power and there was a dim light from a few ceiling ports. At the end of the quay, he turned left into a square-sectioned tunnel and followed it for a good three hundred metres before the way was blocked by a ribbed concrete seal.

Karl said, "It's some time since I was down this way. Last time, it was dry as a bone, but we should be ready to drop this slab, if there's water behind it." He indicated a recess in the tunnel wall with two stub levers, one green and one red. He heaved down on the green one and there was a deep rumble as a massive counterweight took the strain. He said, "Now it should lift. The red lever disengages the counterweight. That's the one, if the sea comes in."

Lined up along the face, they pushed with their palms flat. The slab trembled and moved. Seconds later it had retracted into the roof. Ahead was the quayside of a second dock with the glint of seawater in it and a few scattered wall lights to show them what it was all about.

On the quayside, a long row of torpedolike submersibles lay on a gravity conveyor, ready to be pushed down for launching into the pool. Carter climbed on the conveyor and settled himself astride one of the craft. There was provision for two operators, each with a back rest and a small console set in the deck. He checked around, throwing switches. There was no joy; the machinery was dead.

Karl said, "Wait," and went over to an equipment bay set in the quay wall. He returned with a massive brace and shoved a spade-shaped bit into a slot in the decking, forward of the leading seat. A couple of turns and he lifted off a metre-long section of the deck itself.

Bergman whistled as he looked inside. "Very compact. Very neat indeed. A good piece of design, that. Do you see that, John? Not unlike the strike craft we developed for Western Naval Intelligence. We had the problem of finding a power source that could not be picked up by sonar probes."

Koenig thumped the cowling. "No use to us, unless we know what made them tick. What about it, Karl? Did you ever have one mobile?"

Karl seemed to be debating how far he should go. Finally, he must have decided that having brought the Alphans this far, there was no point in being evasive at the last. He returned to the bay and brought out a grey canister. He said, "My brother is the specialist.

He reckoned it was a type of rocket propulsion. As you see, there's a cradle to take one of these."

It took Bergman ten minutes to sort out the angles. Meantime, Koenig had rooted about in a second equipment bay and came out with a set of skin-diving gear. His nebulous idea of a foray against Caster was crystallising out into a hard-edged plan. He asked, "Did I hear right? Is there a pool on the ground floor?"

Karl said, "Surely. We use it all the time. It's been the best way to keep in shape."

"Could we get a couple of these gizmos upstairs for a trial?"

"No problem."

"Just supposing we make them work, how do we get out of here into the estuary?"

"There's an exit lock. That works for sure. There was a time when some of the youngsters had an aqualung club. But the tides are tricky. There was an accident and two were drowned. The council, in their wisdom, closed them up. Rhoda was in it, as I recall."

Bergman and Carter had fixed the canister in place and connected some valve gear. Carter tried the console again. There was a muted thud as he hit an ignition sequence. Telltales glowed on the hooded console. They were in business.

It took an hour to transport two strike craft to the pool and there was a full set of off-duty Outfarers to watch Koenig and Carter in wet suits and flippers take them through their paces in the huge, indoor swimming bath. They were easy. Very flexible and responsive. By nightfall, Koenig reckoned he was ready for a sea trial.

He met with an ultimatum from the research team. Helena said, "As I see it, you need me along. I'm beginning to see how to go ahead on this neutralising business, but quantities would be critical and it would matter how and where it was introduced in the cycle. I'd have to see how they operate. Count me in, or I can't guarantee any success."

Rhoda said, "*And* me. You need a guide. I've been

along the coast. As a practice, we could go along to where your Eagle came down."

Koenig was not one to stand out against a logical argument. He said, "First light in the morning, then. We'll get these craft refuelled and leave them ready on the quay." With his mind on load and a programme to work on, he was feeling more settled; but as he stood by Karl's shattered observation window and looked out on the night sky of Megaron, he knew he was only going through the motions. He was first and last a spacefarer. His destiny was out there, where Earth's moon was still a brilliant extra on the star map.

Helena Russell moved quietly behind him and put her hands on his shoulders. "A penny for them."

"You'd be paying too much."

"I'm sorry, John."

He turned to face her. "Sorry for what? What did I ever want except a place where we could start again? Now, if I were here and you were on Moonbase Alpha, you could be sorry for me."

He was doing his best, but she knew him too well to be entirely deceived. "That's a nice thing to say to me. But will you ever really be satisfied with what we have here?"

"What is happiness, Helena? I know enough to be sure that nobody can define the terms and say that when such and such a thing is done, they will be happy. It has a knack of turning into dead sea fruit. I reckon it has to be a by-product of something else. If we work at it, here, we might find that it's crept up on us unawares. And for me, at least, all the ingredients are on the site."

She let it go at that. There was no point in persuading him that he ought to be miserable. They linked arms and walked slowly to their own quarters.

Rhoda proved her worth for a team place in the first half hour of the dummy run. She had a quick grasp of procedures and remembered, exactly, the sequences for operating the exit locks from the strike-craft pens. There was an intercom system, which had

been used by the aqualung club, and she brought one
of the ex-members along to stay on the quay to open
up on the return leg. He was a man of her own age
group, Melas, very dark and intense. As the two craft
rode side by side at the entrance to the lock, he said,
"Just in case anybody else is floating around out there,
trying to get in, we should have a code word——
'resurge,' it is. Give me a test call as soon as you get
out into the channel."

Koenig waved Carter to move forward. There was
room for both craft to lie in line astern in the narrow
chamber. The gate closed behind them. Lamps on their
helmets lit the surface, which churned white as water
jetted in from a hidden sluice. Following the manual,
they cleared pressure by thumping hard against a
closed nose. Then the outer gate began to lift and
Carter, with Rhoda riding pillion, edged forward into
four metre's depth of clear water lit by open sky above.

As they fed in power and moved slowly ahead,
Koenig called, "Resurge. Do you read me?"

Melas answered, "Loud and clear, Commander."

"We are moving out into the channel. Stand by."

"Check, Commander."

Koenig took his strike craft ahead of Carter's and
held course for a hundred metres, keeping his distance
from a sloping seabed of pale brown sand. Overhead,
the sea surface was still as a sheet of ridged Duralumin
foil.

Helena Russell, plugged in on a communications
link through the two consoles, spoke intimately into
Koenig's ear. "Water temperature's no problem, John.
We could stay in this all day."

"I'd like to know what can be seen from the surface,
turbulence or air trail." He switched to the general net
to bring in Carter. "Alan?"

"Commander?' '

"I'm going up. Checking on how you look from
above. Just slow ahead and I'll rejoin."

"Check. In water this clear, we'll need more depth
to be hidden from air survey."

"True. But the sea's a big place. They'd have to know where to look."

Koenig broke through the luminous skin of the sea and the sun was a tangible warmth on their heads and shoulders. They were further out from the coast than they expected and from zero level, there was only a limited horizon. The agunt thumb of the tower block dominated the low-lying tip of the peninsula. Only the higher crests of the sand dunes could be seen. A broad belt of trees succeeded the dunes, the remnant of the forest which had once covered the whole area and was slowly winning its way back.

Below them, Carter's craft was a moving shadow, leaving no surface trace. There was no doubt about it. They had the transport side of the operation all buttoned up.

Koenig spent fifteen minutes on practice dives, then, with both craft on the surface and out of sight of land, he went for a speed trial. Opened full out, the two craft tore away side by side. It was exhilarating, a kind of holiday treat. With an eye on the fuel gauge, he called a halt.

"Hold it there, Alan. Slow ahead and pick up the course."

Carter's "Check" was followed by a second transmission as his strike craft continued to tear away over the sea. "She's not answering. Stuck on open throttle. I'll circle."

Koenig and Helena were hove to, rocking gently in the troughs as Carter made a long sweep round them. His voice sounded disgusted. "No joy, Commander. She won't shut down. In fact, she's building up more urge. The power needle's over beyond 'max.' We can run her out and then tow in or let her beach herself."

Koenig was watching. It was true enough, the strike craft was pulling out more speed by the second. The nudge of a sixth sense alerted him. He said, "Alan, can you get clear? Get Rhoda away now. Then set a course for open sea and get clear yourself. We'll pick you up. Do it now."

They heard Rhoda say, "But I *like* it. Why do I have to get off?"

"Because I say so. Stand up. Dive out to the rear but not right over the jets. Right?"

"Say please."

"As God's my witness, I'll turn her out with you still sitting there. Get on with it."

"You're a very hard man, Alan. I don't know why I bother."

They saw her haul herself to her feet, balance for a brief count and plunge clear. Carter was quicker. The strike craft came round in a turn as he altered course and he was on his feet and away before she had settled to the new line.

The two shipwrecked submariners hung on either side of Koenig's strike craft, where grab handles had been provided by the designers. They were too low in the water to see the other streaking away for the horizon. But they could hear the explosion when she pulled a trick not on the maker's manifest.

There was a percussive smack as though a sting ray had slapped down on the sea; a tall plume of water and spray flowered briefly and fell away. There was a single thread of black smoke tinged with a crimson flare and then it was all over. The sea was empty to the horizon. The strike craft had gone.

Alan Carter was no stranger to test runs with a risk surcharge, but he was aggrieved about this one. He said, "But I went through that panel with a tooth comb. There was nothing in the mechanism to do that. She was answering sweet as a nut on the trials."

Koenig said, "That was last night. It stayed out on the quay until we picked them up this morning. I suppose any engineer could have fixed it to do that. Unless it's a freak failure."

Rhoda said indignantly, "What are you suggesting, Commander? My friends would not do that. Even supposing they would do it to *you*, they would not do it to *me*."

Carter lifted himself out of the water to lean over

the hull and pat her shiny head. "True, my flower, but there has to be some explaining done. There was a fail-safe relay on the power feed. Not only did the control fail to respond, but the relay failed to trip. What about this one, Commander?"

"We'll take it slowly. I don't fancy swimming all the way."

"Do we still try to reach Eagle Seven?"

"Not this trip. That water spout might bring company. Before we move off, all hands take a look at this craft. If we have a saboteur at work, he might have a second shot in his locker."

The underside of the hull was a one-piece pressing with a line of shallow, circular depressions to give rigidity and strength. Lying on his back, Koenig finned slowly along its length. He was on a second trip before the pattern registered. The second hollow from the stern held a feature which had no practical purpose. Sited dead centre and looking innocent enough, there was a plate-sized disk. Intakes for the buoyancy tanks were amidships. Fuel recharge and maintenance hatches were on the deck head. He anchored himself to a lug, shone his helmet lamp on the disk and stared at it.

Seen close, it had two parts. The outer cover was set to a flange marked round the rim in fractions of a degree. There was an idented arrow on the rim of the cover and, unless it was a ripple in the water, it flipped a whole gradation as he watched. Three more intervals to go and there was a matching arrow incised on the rim.

Koenig said urgently, "Everybody move away. Keep together."

Habits of obedience moved them off. Even Rhoda reacted to the tone without putting up an argument. He drew a flat-bladed knife from the belt of his diving suit and slid it along the hull under the rim of the device. There was a bubble of released air and before he could catch it, the disk was away, spinning and turning as it dropped through the clear water. He

heaved himself into the saddle, fed in a little power
and moved the strike craft after the swimmers. When
he caught up, he leaned over and heaved Helena
aboard by her harness straps. He said, "Alan, get
yourself out of the water. Rhoda behind Helena, you
up in front here on the bow. As quick as you like."

Rhoda was halfway home, draped over the stern
like a comely, black sack, when the sea erupted and a
metre-high shock wave dipped the craft's cone in a
dive that was out of control. When Koenig finned
powerfully for the surface in a welter of churning water
and sand, his first thought was that the strike craft
had bought it and that without its small chart spread
and directional gear they would have a fifty-fifty
chance of swimming towards the distant polar continent. Then he saw its black stern lift in a swell, almost a hundred metres away. Helena broke surface
close beside him and it was all he wanted to know. He
was away in a racing crawl after their lifeline.

Where there had been just an outside chance that a
machine left in store for so long could develop a fault,
there was no doubt at all that a deliberate hand had
set the limpet mine. It cleared the air in one way.
They knew for a truth they would have to watch their
backs at all times. Rhoda was bitterly ashamed and
could only repeat again and again, "Who would do
such a thing? And why? Why would they do it?"

There was no good answer to be had out in the bay.
Carter and Rhoda trailed like paravanes and the strike
craft cruised at half speed on the surface. Koenig, jaw
set in a grim line, considered the angles. The only
good to come out of the exercise was that somebody
had shown their hand. He was still convinced that he
had a workable plan. Next time he would leave without publicity. He called the pens.

"Resurge. Come in."

Melas answered evenly, without any trace of surprise. It was unlikely that he was the one. "Resurge. I
read you."

"We're coming in."

"Professor Bergman to speak with you."

"Put him on."

Bergman's voice came on the net. "John, there's been an air car roaming about for the last hour. Not attacking. I'd say it was on reconnaissance. Looks like a two-man crew. It's been going low over the estuary, out to sea for a kilometre or so, then back over the same ground. If it wasn't impossible, I'd say he was looking for you."

"Thank you, Victor. Believe me, it isn't impossible, but keep that to yourself. Where is he now?"

"There's an operations room down here that you didn't see. I have a picture of the estuary. He's just turned and he's going along the seawall and heading out to sea. If you're on the surface, you'll see him in about two minutes."

"Thanks, Victor. Over and out."

The twisted spire of the tower block was in sight but the dunes and the shoreline were still over the curve of the sea. Koenig held on for another hundred metres and then killed power. He said, "Hear this. There's a scout out looking for us. He might as well find us. We'll see what he makes of it if we leave the strike craft for him to see. Dive down and make like fish."

From ten metres down, the submersible looked like a black log breaking into the shiny roof. They gripped wrists and stood on the sea floor, looking up like a sea anemone. It seemed a long time. Helena Russell believed that they might take root, grow algae, suffer a sea change into black coral. Then a shadow passed over the surface and a bland, silvery oval shoved itself through the roof of their world and the air car had landed beside the strike craft.

Koenig transferred Helena's wrist to Rhoda's hand, tapped Alan Carter on his chest harness and pointed up. They reached the underbelly of the car at the same time and Koenig, fending off with his finger tips, traversed to the starboard quarter where the strike craft lay alongside. He felt the car dip, as a crewman left the copilot squab and moved aft to open a hatch.

When the man leaned out to grab for a lug on the strike craft decking, the Alphan's face was swimming up to meet him like a bizarre reflection of his own.

For a couple of seconds he was checking it out, too surprised for clear speech, and time ran out for him. Koenig had surged out of the water, grabbed the extended arm and plucked him through the open hatch like some loose-fitting cork.

The pilot, half turned on his chair, was watching the action with one hand drumming on the console. Control had told him to check out the sea approaches and liquidate any Outfarers playing marine games. There were none about. All the euphoric drugs in the world could not stop his digestive clock. He wanted to be back on station where a certain neat-handed Phyllis was keeping it hot for him. When his partner slipped away with waving legs into the drink, he stopped drumming and thumped the release stud of his harness.

A voice from the panel said, "Come in Car Three Nine."

"Three Nine. Pilot Gara."

"Report."

"Investigating a torpedo craft at the mouth of the estuary. Hold it. I have to see what that fool Max is doing."

"Very well."

Gara reached the hatch as Max's EEG went flat. He was floating face down in the space between the craft. The pilot considered it. There was no other movement, except the slow drift of the corpse out of the channel. He was uneasy. Something did not jell. Without his load of tranquillising serum, a simple instinct of self-preservation would have been enough, but he leaned out and grabbed for Max's nearest ankle. It was proof that in the long term, the life force in Caster was following a self-defeating path. Carter took his wrist in a double grip and heaved him out. There was a short, brutal flurry that could only have one end. Carter was still incensed at the thought that Rhoda had been within a fraction of being torn apart by the exploding strike craft.

As Gara joined Max in a slow sarabande round the stationary craft, the two watchers below finned up to the surface. Koenig was already aboard the car. He leaned down and pulled Helena through the hatch, then Rhoda. He called Carter. "Alan. Get on the net. Don't mention the car. Say we're still working out here. We won't be in for a time yet. Tell him to keep on listening watch."

Helena Russell had taken off her face mask and was shaking out her hair. Her eyes were bright and indignant. "You *killed* those men. Did you *have* to do that?"

"They would have killed us."

"But they're not *responsible* for their actions."

"How would you explain that to your wandering spirit if it had been you drifting out there in the sea?"

"I don't know, but it still isn't right. One wrong doesn't make another wrong acceptable."

It was an argument that could have gone on. The control panel spoke up. "Come in Car Three Nine. Pilot Gara. Report."

Koenig scooped up the mike which Gara had left dangling. Funnelling his mouth with his hands for a muffled effect, he said, "Gara."

"Leave the underwater craft. We now know it has been mined. Take one more circuit of the Outfarers' complex and come in. Acknowledge."

"Received. Out."

Rhoda was incredulous. "What can it mean? Is there somebody from Caster on the inside? Why should there be a traitor amongst the Outfarers? Everybody joins from choice and conviction."

Koenig had enough imponderables for his computer to work on. From the pilot seat of the air car, he could see the shoreline. There was still something to be made of the mission and he reckoned the car might be a worthwhile ace to hide away.

He said, "All hands get to work. I want the uniforms off of those zombies. Then we take both craft over to the shore, where the trees come down to the water."

There was a slow burn from Helena Russell and a near mutiny. But finally she joined Carter and they heaved Gara into the freight bay and stripped off his black tunic and pants. In the breast pocket, he carried a folder and when she flipped it open, there was a head-and-shoulders picture of a dark, smiling girl and a caption in a round feminine hand. She passed it to Rhoda. "What does it say?"

" 'I'll be waiting, Phyllis.' "

It was another black mark for Koenig. But he was unrepentant. He said, "She has my sympathy. I'm only glad we don't have hers."

"You're turning into a savage. Or perhaps you always were one under civilisation's veneer?"

"For every activity there is an appropriate mode."

"What's that supposed to mean?"

"It means launch that one on the bosom of the ocean and get busy with the other one."

When it was done, he had sorted the operating panel of the air car and was ready to move. He said, "Take the strike craft, Alan, and follow me in. We'll land at the point."

The tide was coming in and there was a metre of water right up to the tree line. With the strike craft hidden under overhanging branches, Koenig put the two women ashore. He said, "Give us thirty minutes by the clock. If we're not back, go for the pens."

Before they could argue, he was moving off with Carter beside him. He hugged the coast, with the air car at zero height. It was Pullman travel after the strike craft, and ten of his minutes had gone when he picked out the tail of Eagle Seven, still poking up from the dunes.

Carter had already shrugged into a uniform jacket and was ready to go out. He said, "What are we looking for, Commander?"

"Lasers in the weapon rack. Whip out the communi-

cations panel. Victor might be able to fix it. Who
knows? We might get a farewell message through to
Alpha."

They did better. In a concentrated burst, they transferred survival stores, chart manuals, the communica-
tor module, a medical kit complete with a spectrum
analyser and four heavy-duty lasers left in the rack.
Koenig reckoned, soberly, it put them a little way
ahead. They were that much less dependent on the
goodwill of the Outfarers.

On the return leg, he gunned the motors and swept
into the hideaway as Helena was checking her time
disk and debating whether or not to give Genghis Khan
another minute of leeway.

There was room for the car in the overhang and
they moored it fore and aft. The sun was almost vertical overhead as the strike craft slipped back into the
estuary and lined up for the entry channel.

Koenig called, "Resurge. Do you read me?"

"Resurge. Come in."

"We're on the way. Entering the channel now. Prepare to activate the lock."

As they waited, he said, "Hear this, one and all. No
mention of the car. No mention of the mine. Mechanical failure on one craft. With a bit of luck, the saboteur will show his hand."

CHAPTER FIVE

Victor Bergman did his best to keep the conversation going, but it was an unusually quiet meal. Finally, he jacked it in and concentrated on his nut cutlet simulate, with two veg and a piquant heliotrope sauce. His usual ally, Helena Russell, was still pondering on Koenig's new rose as an executioner. Tough and determined, she knew him to be; but ruthless and cold blooded was something else. She looked at him now and again as though at a stranger. When it came down to it, another person, however well known, was finally an enigma.

Rhoda was silent because she could not get over the sabotage bit. It had undermined her sense of security. Somebody she knew well had been instrumental in setting it up and she was going over the list. The vote had shown that the Alphans were not everybody's friend, but she herself was on the home team. Who could have done that to her?

Since she was silent, Carter held his peace with a kind of instinctive sympathy. The only therapy he could think of was out of place in mixed company.

Koenig himself hardly noticed the atmosphere. He was following a complicated line of thought. The existence of a fifth column in the Outfarers' enclave explained some things. With their overwhelming strength, the high command in Caster could have overrun the place anytime they liked to do it. But they had held off. The plant on the inside was the

answer. They were prepared to let the Outfarers flour-
ish, provided they knew what they were getting up to.
It was clever stuff. If the more free-thinking community produced anything that was likely to be of
value, they would get the benefit of it. In some ways,
they were running an experimental farm or a control
group to monitor their own manipulated society.

But who would do that? On the face of it, such an
idea would be outside the scope of people who were
all regimented by the authoritarian Spadec organisation. Unless Spadec was outside its own control
machinery? That was too difficult to take any further
and he shifted to another angle. If there was an in-
former, constantly in touch with Caster, how was it
that Karl's jailbreak plan had succeeded?

With an effort, he shifted over to practicalities. It
was still good thinking to carry the war into the Spadec
camp. The sooner the better. One thing stood out a
good sea mile: the fewer people who knew about it,
the better. He said to Helena, "You think you can
crack it?"

It was a tribute to her intuition that she knew what
he was on about. "The drug? Not a doubt. With the
analyser I can cut corners."

"You haven't shown that to anybody?"

"Not yet. But whoever's in the lab is bound to be
curious. Manufacturing the neutralising agent will be
the tricky part."

"I'd like to have it just as soon as it's possible."

"Then the sooner I go to work, the better."

He was not to be allowed an easy ride back into
full-citizen status in the Russell book; but he could be
stubborn himself and reckoned he had nothing to apol-
ogise for. "Right, then. I'll be working at the pens.
Give me a signal as soon as you like. Victor can help
you with it. Alan and Rhoda with me."

Before he went below, he made a call on Karl. The
Outfarers' leader was mobilising all hands to restore
the damaged apartments. It would have been possible
to leave them and shift into other accommodation,

but it would have been bad for morale. Without being an expert, Karl was a practical psychologist of the old school and knew by instinct what was best for community health.

Koenig took him aside. "That foray into Caster——to spring Rhoda—took some planning. Was it a council decision?"

"There's a small management group. We worked it out."

"But everybody knew what you were doing?"

"Most people. What are you getting at, Commander?"

"Just following a thought. I get the feeling, after today's trip, that Spadec might know more than you think about what goes on here. Would they know about a beamed monitor system?"

"It means nothing to me. What would that be?"

Koenig let it pass. He went on. "You fixed a plan, fixed a time and carried it through?"

"You've either said too much or too little. What are you getting at, Commander?"

"Was that the way it was?"

Karl hooked his thumbs in his belt and stood four-square, a solid, capable figure. He gave Koenig a straight look. "Not quite like that. I knew it had to be foolproof and I was moving slowly to get everything right. Then I got anxious about what might be happening to Rhoda and I brought the whole thing forward by twenty-four hours. I only wish now it had been earlier. It might have saved her some grief. Was that what you wanted to know?"

Years of operating in the command slot told Koenig that whoever might be the plant, it was not Karl. He said, "That was what I wanted to know, and I believe now that if you'd waited and gone the distance, you'd have found a reception party waiting for you."

Karl said, "That's hard to accept. But I can see that you believe it to be true. There's no harm in being on guard for the future." He looked thoughtfully at the Outfarers, who were busy collecting shards of plexiglass into disposal bins. If any likely names had risen in his head, he was keeping them there. He went on. "This has a bearing on your mission. Can you go ahead, believing that you could be walking into a trap?"

"There is a difference. For one thing, it isn't widely known what we intend to do. For another, there was no time set."

"Then we should keep it that way. Don't even tell me."

"But you agree that the attempt should be made?"

"It's a positive step forward and might do good. I'll defend it in the council. But you saw the vote. There's a strong conservative element for no change. It could make you look like dangerous partners to have."

"We'll take that risk. As of now, we're going down to the pens to fuel a couple of strike craft. As soon as Doctor Russell is ready, we'll move."

"Melanion will need to know or you won't have any power down there."

"Just Melanion, then. With Rhoda involved, he should be safe enough."

Karl turned away a shade too quickly and went to rejoin the chain gang.

Down at the pens, Koenig and Carter checked over four strike craft and fitted them with fuel canisters. Two they manhandled down the slipway on launching buggies; two they left on the conveyor with nothing to indicate that they had been prepared for use.

It was all they could do. The ball was in Helena's court. The next step was up to her. Rhoda and she met them as they closed the seal to the dock complex and there was no doubt about what she had to report.

She said simply, "It wasn't too difficult. As it turns out, I've met something very like it before. Quantities are very small. By itself it wouldn't amount to much, but it would predispose a subject to react to suggestions."

Carter said, "It sounds like a good idea."

She ignored him, but Rhoda gave him a wide-eyed look and said "Only think. . . ."

Helena went on. "It was used as a preparation for hypnosis therapy, only in a much stronger form. The way it is, I can synthesise an additive that breaks it down into two harmless components. I'd guess that they have a drip input to the protein silos. There's no technical problem at all."

Koenig asked, "When can you have the additive ready?"

"Give me one hour and there'd be enough to neutralise a year's supply."

"A year ought to be long enough. Well done, apothecary."

"Don't patronise me."

"Nothing was further from my mind."

Twilight on Megaron, in the seaboard zone, was a short and dramatic switch from bright day to velvet, black night. Photosensitive relays tripped in the Outfarers' complex and house lights brightened in the living quarters. There was a tradition of making a long and leisurely evening meal. Children came in from the day-care service and the community broke down into nuclear units.

The overall atmosphere was settled and domestic and at odds with the Alphans' preparation for a move in the hot war. Gelanor, on good-neighbour principles, had them in for supper and being a compulsive talker, was probably the only one who missed the undercurrents of strain. Melanion, dark, thin faced and given to introspection, was very different from his brother and seemed an unlikely consort for her. He listened and said little.

Victor Bergman said, "I can see that the Outfarers can only move slowly. But in Caster, you have the manpower and resources for an expansion programme. I don't understand this deliberate holding back. How can a society stay static for so long?"

Karl said, "You have to understand the history of

Megaron. In the past, we pushed to the frontiers of knowledge. When you think of it, all that could be discovered had been discovered and lost. Probably more than once. It's a waiting time. A period of lying fallow."

Helena said, "Fine, if it's done from choice. But as we see it, this is enforced by Spadec, and Spadec isn't too particular how it uses people. Where was the sense in the suicide attacks on our Eagle? It only needed a little communication to establish that we were on a peaceful mission."

Breaking a long silence, Melanion said, "So you say. But your mission was to bring a big group of Alphans to Megaron. Who is to say whether that was for the long-term good or not?"

Koenig asked, "What do you believe?"

"It is of no importance what I believe. I am saying how it could look to those being invaded by an alien craft."

Returning to his theme, Bergman said, "As I understand it, the situation has been unchanged for some hundreds of years. That is a long time, even for an ancient race. Earth Planet is newly civilised by comparison with Megaron, but taking the last three centuries, we could point to a scale of change and progress that has transformed the way of life for millions of people. Once across the technological barriers, the sky's the limit for human aspirations."

"But do people change so much, Victor?" Helena was on a hobbyhorse. "Technology is only the tip of the iceberg. It took millions of years of development to produce *homo sapiens*. He can't cut loose from his past. All his drives and instincts relate to the evolutionary period. Even here, I'd guess that there was no essential difference between the people of Caster and their ancestors who built this tower city, or, for that matter, from those who were on this site, chipping at trees with an adze."

It could have gone on a long time. Koenig caught Karl's eye and the Outfarer took the hint. He said, "I know our Alphan friends have work to do. Don't stand on ceremony, Commander. Feel free to go. I, for one, go along with what Doctor Russell was saying. I'd go further. It seems to me that there are no real differences between *Alphans* and ourselves. Once intelligent life has gotten off the ground, it faces the same problems everywhere and, for the most part, comes up with the same answers."

He joined them in their apartment and looked at the litre can of colourless liquid that Helena had brought in from the lab. "This is it, then?"

"If we can get it where it will do some good."

"Doing good by stealth. Who knows what good is?"

Koenig said, "Not entirely for their good, as you understand. It puts their future back in their own hands, gives them freedom to think and more to do than harass the Outfarers."

Bergman said, "There's one possibility we haven't considered, John. Freedom to choose is freedom to choose badly. They could be more militant and not less."

"It hasn't worked out that way for the Outfarers."

"True. But it's a curious position in ethics. Spadec doesn't ask whether they *do* want the social drug. We are not asking whether they *do not* want it."

Koenig was already seeing the dark waters of the estuary and reckoned that any more philosophy would be counterproductive. He said quietly, "It's tonight, Karl. We can't afford to wait for our intentions to leak across to Caster. Who can you trust to be on standby at the pens?"

"Do you trust me?"

"Yes."

"Then I'll be there. Who goes?"

"Captain Carter, Doctor Russell, Rhoda, myself."

"Does it have to be Rhoda?"

"She's a volunteer. She's had some experience with the strike craft and she knows the ground."

"What time?"

"Twenty-three hundred."

"Very well, then."

"Professor Bergman will keep watch with you."

"Right. I'll set it up. I find it strange, that something so important to Megaron should have to wait for strangers to carry it through."

"The onlooker sees most of the game."

"It could be so."

To all appearances, the vast, ruined tower was deserted when the Alphans walked quietly through the corridors and dropped to the underground dock system. Karl had provided hand-powered vibrators to make up the tool kit. Koenig and Carter had lasers in the waterproof pouches of their diving gear. Helena's litre of reagent had been divided into four handy flasks to clip on their belts.

There was no opposition. No problem. At the dock, Koenig ignored the strike craft already launched and brought down the two left on the conveyor. On visual check, there had been no sabotage. They slipped into water, warm from the day's heat. Victor Bergman said, "Good luck, John. Take care. Don't push too hard. If there are snags, leave it. There's always another day."

Beyond the channel, they surfaced below the night sky of Megaron, with Earth's errant moon throwing a silver streak on the wine-dark sea. As they rounded the point, there was a pale aureole over the land to mark out the site of Caster itself. The strike craft ghosted through a flat calm, the human cargo feeling the strangeness of their isolation after the domestic comfort of the enclave.

Helena Russell thought of the Eagles touching down on Moonbase Alpha and the Alphans filing back into the empty rooms. There would be a reshuffle in the command chain. Mathias would have taken her slot as head of the medical services. Life would go on. It was like a foretaste of death and they were here in a fair mock-up of the traditional idea of limbo. They had to work their passage to a rebirth. In those terms, what Koenig was doing made a kind of sense.

The man himself had enough navigational problems to keep his mind on load. The gaunt sentinel of the tower block and the arc of Caster's lights gave him a fix. He had memorised the line of the coast and could visualise where the wreck of Eagle Seven was stuck in the dunes and the location from there of the hydroponic farm spread.

He had a moment's self-doubt. Here he was, fresh on the scene, where men had been living out their time for untold centuries, taking a hand in a social engineering job which they could have done for themselves if they had wanted it. This was the sin of arrogance that the gods slapped down.

Then he remembered the air cars streaking in to destroy Eagle Seven. It had to be done. Every man wanted to see progress in his own time. They could not wait in the wings and hope for a miracle.

He twisted in the saddle and looked at Helena. What he could see of her face was pale as marble. "All right?"

"Yes."

"Here we go, then." He changed course and the strike craft began to dip and lift through a long swell as they bored in for the distant beach.

Closer in, there was the suck and slide of shingle and they beached the strike craft, one at a time, on a flat, stony strip that pushed out into the sea in a long tongue. Further up the beach, they discarded life-support gear, replaced flippers with black foam-soled sneakers and climbed the first dune, four dark shadows melding into darkness.

At the top, they lay flat in a row. It was all there. Eyes adjusted to a low lumen count, they could see the farm spread stretching away in all directions. Close at hand, it looked huge.

At the bottom of the slope, there was a two-metre-high chain-link fence that surrounded the complex. Inside, the culture tanks were set out as long, shallow concrete throughs, each about three metres wide and thirty metres long. The long sides carried rails, and a trolley, with a seat and operating gear, straddled the trough. It could be pumped along the track by a hand lever and the farmer could go along dumping nutrients in the growing medium or harvesting his crop.

Dotted about on a regular plan were white-painted silos. In the centre was a squat, hexagonal tower; three floors; dark below and with lights from two windows at the top. Mineral tracks from the silos led to it like spokes to the hub of a wheel. Rhoda pointed and breathed, "That's the control centre. Final processing will be done there. We do this on a small scale. The end product is a protein pellet. That's the staple. All the food's made from that. Except fruit. Fruit we grow by itself. There's a kind of fruit we use to make bread—"

Koenig held up his hand. It was all good, interesting stuff, but better at another time. He said, "Alan. Go down and take a look at that fence."

Carter was away, hardly visible until he appeared again as a dark shape against the mesh. He was less than a minute before he came back up the dune. "No problem, Commander. I tried one strand. This vibrator goes through like a hot knife in butter. No electrification."

They took out a metre-long panel and rolled it back. One by one, they slipped through. Koenig meticulously refixed the wire, so that only the most careful check would locate the break. Between the troughs, there was a paved strip and they went along in single file, Koenig in the lead with his laser set for a stun beam and Carter bringing up the rear.

They were halfway to the centre, when Koenig stopped and went down on one knee. A moving light had separated out from the pale glow of Caster and was coming towards them on a course that would cross the farm. Behind it was the familiar shadow of an air car.

As it came nearer, a pencil of light probed out from

the cone and lit up the distant area of the farm beyond
the tower. Koenig said, "Down," and flattened himself against the side of the trough. His mind raced
through the possibilities. It could be a routine patrol,
or it could be that there had been a signal from the
Outfarers. If the last, there was only Karl with precise
information. Unless there was electronic monitoring
that even Karl was not aware of.

There was action from the tower. A light went on
in the ground floor and then the whole area turned
to bright day. Floods on a high gantry made a brilliant
line. Seen clear, there was a paved apron on two sides
of the tower and a parking lot with half a dozen
freight carriers in line. The final delivery from
the farm to Caster itself was made by an air-shuttle
service.

The incoming car swept into the pool of light,
hovered and dropped on its hydraulic jacks close to
the building. It was a personnel carrier. Its lights went
out, the hatch opened and a black-coated Megaronian
climbed onto the pad. It was the farmer, home from a
night out in the big city. His progress was slow and er-
ratic. He had done well to steer a course for home.

As he opened a door, the outside lights snapped
out and he was silhouetted in the opening. Koenig
was on his feet and padding forward at a run. They
reached the wall of the control centre as the down-
stairs lights went out.

The door was flush fitting, with no visible means of
opening it from the outside. Koenig moved off to circle
the building. In the centre of the face, there was
a hinged flap where the track from a silo made its entry. Dumper trucks would push their way through. He
went on hands and knees in the centre of the track
and shoved. It was open. He said, "Very carefully.
There's no prize for ending up as a protein pellet."

The warning was timely. They were moving from
dim light into the blackness of a pit. On hands and
knees, Koenig checked out the ground by touch. The
rails on either side were continuous. He tried to vis-

ualize what would be happening to a truck shunted in through the hatch. There would be some mechanism for emptying it. There would be a self-tipping device. Hands sliding along the rails, he identified holding clips and then another set about half a metre farther on. Why two sets? One would be enough to stop the incoming carrier. What would happen to the load? Not tipped on the deck between the tracks, for a sure thing. There was a slight trembling in the floor and even as it began to tilt away, he had arrived at a theoretical answer. The truck would hit the spring-loaded stops. Its construction would be asymmetrical, so that weight distribution would give it a turning moment round the centre of a pivot. The whole section of floor would swivel and the contents would be dumped on a conveyor or into a tank.

It was nice to have it clear, but he was falling forward. Close behind him, Helena Russell had sensed that he was in trouble and flicked on her lamp. She could see the floor lifting in front of her and Koenig's heels going up. She grabbed for the rising edge and hung on. There was a halt and a moment of stability as mechanical laws tried to sort it out. Koenig himself arched his back and grabbed for the solid floor ahead, shifting his grip a fraction of a second before Helena's weight turned the scale and the revolving flap slammed back in place.

The rising stench from the pit was enough to numb the brain and was still lingering about as he wormed forward in a closed box-section conduit. There was no need to worry about showing a light. The operating principles were clear. Once having dumped its load, the truck would go on and pass out of the factory without seeing the light of day.

Koenig crawled on, looking up at the roof. There had to be an inspection trap for maintenance. He found it, ten metres farther on, and waited for the others to join him. There was a round plate, dropped in a seating, with lugs to engage in a couple of slots.

Lights switched out, he moved it a quarter turn and lifted slowly.

Seen from the inside, the ground floor of the control centre looked much bigger. There were low-power courtesy lights dotted about, giving only a faint glow, but enough to see by.

Koenig lowered the lid to the housing of the conduit, pulled himself through and leaned in to heave Helena through. The conduits themselves divided the floor space into areas and the tops had been developed as work heads. In the centre was a recognisable command island with flow diagrams on freestanding display boards and a whole raft of electronic hardware.

Far over, against an outside wall, there was a long supply bay with labelled bins and hoppers. Nutrients to be issued to the growing tanks. It was not that much different from the supply department for the hydroponics section on Moonbase Alpha, except that it was on a bigger scale. Helena Russell took her time, identifying departments, and then pointed. "Over there, I think, John."

"Take the flasks, then, and see what you can do. Alan, cover down here. I'll take the stairway. Stun beams if anybody shows. With a bit of luck they might not remember what it was all about."

It was surprising to Koenig that the operation was not mounted round the clock. Production must be streamlined during the day to feed Caster's population from this one centre. There was room for a higher yield. Moving silently, he climbed the spiral stairway to the first floor. It was a duplicate of the floor below except that there was no provision for incoming trucks. It was divided two ways. Half was stacked with the plastic sacks beside a gravity conveyor belt. This was the supply reservoir. Perhaps a month in hand? It would be a fair time before the neutralised food began to pass into the supply chain. The rest of the space was reserved for machinery spares and back-up stocks of nutrients.

The spiral stairway went on to the top floor. There was a murmur of voices coming down the well. Koenig crossed to a window and looked out. The bowl of light over Caster had dimmed down. By his time disk, it was 0130. A dark ribbon ran from the perimeter fence of the farm in the direction of the town. Inside the fence, it connected with a broad paved strip coming all the way to the apron of the control centre. So there was a surface road in addition to the air-car link. He was turning away, when a movement caught his eye. Night glasses would have made it clear. As it was, he could not be sure. He padded over to the head of the stairs, dropped down halfway and signalled for Alan Carter to join him. Helena was working with Rhoda at a long preparation trough with carboys on an overhead rack.

Carter put his forehead to the glass and went still as death. There was a slow count of five before he would commit himself. "It's a company on the march. Classic camouflage. No bright metal. Hands and faces black. For us?"

There was no doubt in Koenig's mind. "Surely for us. They've been tipped off."

Even as he spoke, there was a change. The moving shadow on the road was dividing left and right and melding into the darkness. A task force was being deployed to surround the farm. At the same time, there was a melodic pinger sounding on the floor above. It was still going as Koenig appeared head and shoulders out of the well to check the set.

This floor had been developed as a living area for farm staff. The head of the stairs came up into a lounge, with club chairs, small tables, what looked like a bar across one corner and half a dozen archways leading off. A light was winking on a wall console behind the bar and it was from there that the audio signal had its source.

Nobody was keen to answer. Then, close at hand, a woman's voice, sounding surly, said, "What can they want at this time, in the Devil's name? Answer

it, Yatpan. Ring, ring, ring, ring. Do you want everybody out of their bed? You can stir yourself quick
enough to get into Caster to see that vixen, Hella."

"Peace, Zarah. Hold your tongue or I'll still it for
you."

Other doors were opening in the distant reaches of
the floor. The same voice was lifted in a growl. "All
right. I'll see to it!"

It was probably the man who had arrived home
late by air car. He emerged barefoot and wearing only
a green towel tucked round his waist, his hair wet and
plastered to his skull. He had been freshening up in a
shower and was now able to walk a straight course.

It was an interesting sidelight on the system.
Neither the drug nor the subliminal suggestion—if
that was on stream—could guarantee fidelity or make
for universal goodwill. He shoved a stud on the box
and the pinger shut itself off. His voice was no more
friendly as he said, "Tylon is it? What fool trick
is this? Can't it wait until morning? All the lights . . .
all round the boundary? . . . You've got me out of my
bed to switch on all the lights? . . . Whose crazy idea
was that?"

There was a pause as the questioner turned
listener for a spell, and when Yatpan spoke again,
there was a marked difference in his voice. It was still
rough, but it was willing. "Spadec directive two four
for this day. Very well. At once, Tylon. I'll see to that.
Outfarers attacking the farm, you say? They must
have gone out of their minds. We have tolerated them
long enough. It's time Spadec cleared them out. We
should drive them into the sea. I have it clear. Spadec
directive two four for this day."

It occurred to Koenig that he might be getting an
insight into how the system worked. Given a predis-
position to follow instructions and a carrier wave going out continuously to reinforce it, the directing
genius would only need to put in a cue word to trigger
complete hypnotic response. At some stage, the people of Caster could be given individual preparation,

After that, they could be turned loose without strings attached. The code phrase would be "Spadec directive," followed by the serial-number of the order on a daily basis.

Yatpan was now on official business. He looked at his towel, as if debating whether it would be right to throw switches on the master console while in boudoir rig. There was a Spadec directive on file that personnel should be dressed at all times in a manner suited to the activity on hand.

He was still debating it when Koenig shot a stun beam with mathematical precision at the centre of his forehead. Black night filled his eyes and he pitched forward on the thick pile carpet.

There was the sound of light, quick footsteps. Zarah was pushing her luck and coming to investigate. Koenig ducked below floor level. He heard her say, "Yatpan? What did they want? Yatpan. . . ." Another voice asked, "What is it, Zarah?"

"There was a call from Caster. Yatpan answered it and was coming back. The drunken fool's fallen over his own feet. Help me get him to his bed."

There was the light slap of a hand striking skin and Zarah went on. "That's you all over, Alcon. Never miss a trick. Don't mess about. Take his shoulders."

"I'd just as soon dump him down the stairwell. Why don't we do that?"

"Because we wouldn't get away with it, that's why."

Koenig withdrew. Even with a thought-control system, the human scene had its unresolved problems. He met Carter's enquiring eye and pointed down to the lower level. When they were well out of earshot, he said, "It was a call from Caster to light up the complex. We have a temporary holdfast on that, but there's not a doubt they'll call again when they see it isn't being done. It's time to move out."

Helena Russell had fixed every carboy on the rack. She had been right in her theory about how the additive was put into the food chain. A thick slurry from the supply tanks below was sucked by vacuum to the

work tops and mixed with a calculated ration of the
liquid from the carboys. Then it was processed and
progressed through the system to leave at the far end
as convenient-sized pellets of protein material for use
in Caster. There it would be textured and flavoured
to make a variety of different foods. In essence, it was
the same system that had served them well on Moonbase Alpha and was probably the most efficient
method of converting solar energy into human fuel
that could be devised.

Koenig said, "Leave it now, Helena. Time to go and
we have to make it quick."

"I've finished."

"Can anybody tell that you've done it."

"Not without sampling and analysis."

"Let's hope they think we never got this far."

"The flasks are full of liquid we had to take out to
make room for our neutraliser."

"As soon as we get outside, empty them."

The return leg through the conduit was no problem.
Koenig hurried them along. Outside in the starlight,
with Earth's withdrawing moon still a feature of the
night sky, he put himself in the place of the Megaronian commander. He would know that the intruders
had come by sea and would send a detachment ahead
to close that escape route. Very likely, they were already in place. The one direction he would be least
concerned about would be the very road he had
marched along from Caster. So that was the way to
go. Out towards Caster and then in a flanking move
behind the troops, who would be all looking in
towards the farm.

He said, "This way," and led off at a jog trot along
the throughway to the main gate.

CHAPTER SIX

The double-leaf gate of the farm complex opened out-
wards to the Caster road. There was no visible locking
mechanism. Koenig had his hand on a cross beam to
push it open, when the nudge of a sixth sense stopped
him dead. He said, "Check the hinge posts. There
could be a signal to the house.

Rhoda found it on the king post of the principal
leaf. There was a spring-loaded stud, held back by
the hanging stile of the gate. As the gate opened, it
would act as a circuit breaker. Koenig took the pressure with the flat of his knife until the others were
through, then Carter took over.

They followed the road, walking five metres to the
left of it on soft sand, black shadows, hardly visible to
each other. They had the tactical advantage of the
light. The reduced glow from Caster was ahead of
them and behind the Megaronians. Koenig reckoned
that somewhere up the road there would have to be a
picket. It might be an unlikely route, but no commander would ignore it completely. They would be
off the road and in cover. It was all a question of who
saw whom.

They had levelled with the crest of a gradual rise.
Koenig, in the lead, was bent double, to minimise his
silhouette against the sky, when the whole of the farm
spread lit up like a stadium. Tylon, impatient with the
negative response, had tried again. This time, he had

gotten Zarah, who sounded breathless, but willing to cooperate.

There was no need to say it. The Alphan party dropped flat to the sand and crawled the ten metres needed to take them below the top and into the reverse slope. Except for the farm spread itself, which had been dug out to a level, the whole area was crossed by parallel dunes, starting close together and steep near the sea, and gradually smoothing out towards the plain around Caster. At the bottom of the one they were in, they could stand erect and still be screened from the control centre, but at any second a Megaronian could appear on either side. There was no cover.

They had to try. Koenig set a punishing pace, with the drag of the sand holding them back like a sequence in a half-remembered nightmare. From somewhere near the coast, a thin, high whistle shrilled. It was answered by another from way behind them and a third, very much nearer, on their side of the farm. Koenig stopped. Lasers ready, he and Carter covered two arcs. From over the ridge, between them and the sea, there was the chink of metal as somebody hit the stock of a carbine against a clip case. Straining to hear, it was just possible to pick up the scuff of feet as the hidden patrol took off in a dash to surround the farm.

Koenig pointed ahead. For a time, at least, they could afford to walk. Earth's diminishing moon was like a talisman bringing them luck. He could imagine the duty crew in Main Mission watching Megaron. While it was still there in vision, they were somehow part of it. When it finally disappeared, it would be like a door closed on the major part of their lives.

He took them on for the best part of a kilometre before he stopped again. Carter said, "When they draw blank, they'll know we slipped through the net. They'll know we can't get far on foot. I'd say they'll whistle up some cars and do an air search."

Rhoda put an arm round his waist and leaned her

dark head on his shoulder. She said, "If we reach the trees, they won't be able to do that. But walking overland is dangerous even in daylight. Karl says there are pockets of poisoned soil even on the peninsula."

The valley they were in had narrowed and deepened. Koenig went up the side on hands and knees to take a look at the topography. He could pick out glints of water in the sea. The farm-spread complex was out of sight, except for the top floor of the control block and one tall lighting gantry. It was still brilliantly lit. If anything, their line of march had taken them nearer to Caster, which was not good. The dark mass of the forested strip was between them and the Outfarers. Distances on land were deceptive. It had not seemed too far by sea, going in straight lines. In his mind, he had been making for Car Thirty-nine. It was still the best bet. But it was all of four kilometres to the nearest edge of the trees. He noticed the flask hanging at his belt and remembered that it was enough to blow the mission, if they were caught. He said, "Empty the flasks. It's a straight dash for the tree line. But with the luck we're having, it should be in the bag."

Helena Russell thought privately that only an optimist could see it that way. Moving through unfamiliar country, one jump ahead of the posse, with a doubtful welcome at the far end was no way to spend the small hours of a new day. She kept it to herself and fell in behind the leader as Koenig fixed a line by a star cluster and led off across the dunes.

It was a half hour by his time disk, before Koenig called another halt. Progress was slower than he had hoped. A lot of urge had been used up in simply taking them up and down the slopes of fine sand. Sweat and grit, working inside the suits, was rubbing them raw. With or without a pursuit force, it was going to be a physical-endurance marathon. He could not understand why the search had not widened out from the farm. By this time, Mestor, if he was in charge of the operation, must be convinced that the Alphans

were outside the fence and since they had not
returned to the strike craft, they would have to be on
the ground between the farm and their home base.

He gave them two minutes and stood up. There
was no word spoken. What could not be altered had
to be endured. There was a change in the ground. It
was flatter and stonier. They could make better time.
Eyes well adjusted to the starlight, they could see the
black blur of the tree line all the time as a visible goal.
For two kilometres, they pressed on. There was another change. Wind-borne seed from the forest was
working to reclothe the man-made desert and small
clumps of stunted trees were struggling for a foothold.
It was an encouragement, but before they could take
much pleasure in it, there was a setback.

Koenig had seen a dark line crossing the landscape
even from the last dune and had not been able to decide what it might be. They were a hundred metres
from it when Rhoda suddenly said, "Oh, no!"

It was enough to halt the column. Koenig said,
"What is it?"

She said, "I should have remembered. There's a
deep fault running across. It runs all the way down to
the sea. We can only cross it on the beach or way up
beyond Caster."

Koenig could have said: "Now you tell me!" Instead, he nodded. "It would have still been there,
whether you remembered or not. We had to come this
way. Let's take a look."

When they reached the edge, it was clear enough
that Rhoda was right. The land had slipped along a
pressure line and pulled apart for ten metres. Depth
was lost in darkness and the sides were sheer. The far
side was higher than where they stood and it was the
dark face of the rock that had looked like a black line.

Without hesitation, Koenig set off along the edge
towards the sea. It was still the right direction. Ten
minutes later, he stopped again and knelt down to
consider a striking piece of botanical enterprise. A
metre below the rim, a run of topsoil had lodged itself

in a fissure and spilled out on a narrow ledge. A tree had found enough food and shelter to get itself established. The trunk had grown out and then made a ninety-degree switch to take itself up into the light.

Lying flat and leaning over, he used his laser for a slicing cut that filled the air with resinous wood smoke. Still upright, the tree dropped, until the severed trunk hit the ledge. Slowly and then gathering speed, the tip tilted away in an arc and thumped down on the far side. The foot lifted and then settled back. The noise, after the silence, was startling and Koenig knew it would carry a long way. Any advantage would have to be exploited quickly.

He dropped down to the ledge and tried to move the tree. It was solid. Faces in a row looking down at him were sober and considering. It was good thinking in a theoretical sense, but another turn of the screw on a bad night. Waiting would not improve it. He said, "I'll give you a call when I'm over. Keep it going as fast as you like."

There was no big problem. Given more time, he would have trimmed a few branches, but in a half minute he was stepping on solid rock and calling for Helena to follow. He handed her out and waited for Rhoda. On the higher ground, it was easier to look across at the distant farm spread. Pencils of light were crisscrossing outside the lights of the complex itself. The search party had finally gotten itself airborne.

Rhoda arrived and knelt down to look anxiously along the trunk for Carter. As soon as he came through the foliage, they all took a hand to heave on the tip and walk it round until they could dump the tree into the cleft.

Flying low, with searchlights boring down to the ground, the cars were working out towards them in a methodical pattern of search. Koenig pushed up the pace to a jog trot. Every hundred metres the cover was improving. By the time the first pair of cars had reached the fissure, they were in bush thick enough to slow them to a walk. Still getting glimpses of his star cluster, he changed direction and they picked their way through the forest towards the sea.

Progress was impossible to judge. Underfoot, tree roots and thick ferns made every step a hazard. They went on, because there was nothing else to do and nowhere else to go. Occasionally, the lights of a searching car would cut a swathe through the darkness and they froze against tree trunks until it had gone.

Rhoda, weakened by her spell in Caster, was reeling like a drunk, forcing herself to go on, but too stupid with tiredness to protect herself. She was walking into more trees than she missed. Alan Carter caught her on a rebound and put her over his shoulder in a fireman's lift.

There had been no cars overhead for a good five minutes and Helena said, "Can we believe it? Have they given up?"

Koenig called a halt to consider it. Carter stood Rhoda against a tree. She was asleep on her feet. He said, "I doubt it, Commander. My guess is that they'll be lined up on the other side of the forest, waiting for us to show."

Koenig said, "You could be right at that. When we reach the car, we'll float her out and get well away from land before we take her up."

He moved them out to more open ground at the edge of the wood. Carter's analysis was standing up. There was no car in sight. They had checked to that point and moved over. It was easier to cover the ground and they could measure progress with sight and sound of the sea. The last hundred metres of beach was wide open with no scattered cover and they kept close to the tree line, walking in the bed of a shallow gulley, ankle deep in brackish water that drained from the forest. There was only one sure way of finding the car from the land. They would have to wade out round the point and check along the shore for recognition marks.

For that matter, it was a relief to slip into the water and take the weight off their feet. Koenig stood waist deep, cupped his hands and rinsed the sweat and sand off his face. The action cleared his head. He was in danger of thinking the end game would be too easy. For that matter, there was no guarantee that Car Thirty-nine had not already been found.

There had been erosion on the coast. Some trees now had their roots in water at some stages of the tide. There was a powerful bouquet of rotting vegetation and they were disturbing clouds of small midges that settled on any patch of open skin. As they rounded a rocky spur, Koenig held up his hand. For a brief count, he believed the car had slipped her moorings and was drifting out to sea. Then he could make out two shadowy figures through the plexiglass. She was an active unit of the task force doing a quiet survey of the coastline.

There was movement, but it was desperately slow. The Megaronian car was bows on to the beach, making leeway towards the farm. How far they would go before they used power to back off or take up a new station was anybody's guess. Koenig gave them fifty metres, ducked under a floating log and went on slowly. Five minutes later, they were standing beside the hull of Car Thirty-nine.

Carter took the copilot seat and switched on the communications net. Somebody would be master minding the operation and might have information to give. It was Mestor himself in mid-speech and what he was saying related to another action. Since he was spending the night on a duty stint, he had extended his brief. The Outfarers were taking another hammering.

". . . Spadec directive Ninety-five. . . . Squadron Three turn over the estuary and take the seaward side. Maximum penetration into the living quarters. Use incendiary charges. Re-form at three four nine eight seven zero. Make your own way to Security Headquarters and stand down."

There had been more. From close at hand, there was the beat of a motor starting up and a beam of light swept briefly across the sea. The car on watch had taken off, no doubt summoned to share in the strike. Rhoda, who had been lying full length in the rumble, sat up and said, "That is terrible. They are determined to destroy our homes. Where shall we go? If they carry on in this way, the Outfarers are finished. We cannot fight Spadec."

Bitterly, John Koenig assessed his own share. He had jumped in with both feet. Theoretically, what the Alphans had done was right. But was that always enough? He had stirred up a hornets' nest and the Outfarers were on the receiving end of a punitive reprisal they had not invited. He could only hope that alarm systems would stand up and the Outfarers would get themselves to a safe place. He said, shortly, "Cast off. We'll go out to sea. Make a detour. Come in across the estuary."

Car Thirty-nine slipped out of cover, ghosted out, rose to zero height and fled away across the wine-dark sea. When they turned to follow the coast, they could see the twisted ruin of the tower city bathed in a ruby glow. Mestor's strike had already had its effect. Smoke and flame were licking out from the lower floor.

When Koenig brought the car down in the estuary, close to the site of the strike craft entry lock, Mestor's force had gone. The fire at the lowest level of the tower city had either burned out or had been put out. Higher levels were still flaming like a gigantic torch and charred debris was falling from a great height to shatter on the paved surrounds or plummet into the sea.

Koenig said, "Use the strike craft frequency, Alan. See if you can talk to Victor."

Carter was less than a minute setting it up. Then he was speaking on the net with Rhoda leaning over the squab and breathing emotionally down his neck. "Resurge. Strike craft calling Outfarers. Come in, Outfarers."

There was no reply. Helena said, "Could it be that they suspect a trap? Or are they all dead?"

Carter called again. "Resurge. Do you read me? Come in, Outfarers."

Rhoda said, "Professor Bergman would recognise your voice. But perhaps he is not there. Let me try."

Even through the filter of the electronic gear, there would be no mistaking the vibrations of her warm, brown tones. She said, "Resurge. We are back. All safe. But what has happened to you? Karl, it's me, Rhoda. Please answer."

This time, there was progress. But it was not Karl's voice. She said, "It's Melanion. It's my father."

He sounded less than pleased. "Resurge. We hear you. So you have returned. Look around you. Can you expect a welcome? Can we allow you to put more lives at risk? You must wait until we decide what is to be done."

There was enough truth in it to be uncomfortable. But Koenig could see the faces of his companions in the glow of the burning tower. They had run a taut mission and soldiered on without complaint. There was nothing wrong with the theory that had set them to work. Their success had gone sour, but it was a calculated risk. They deserved better than a brush-off. He said harshly, "Commander Koenig. Let me speak with Professor Bergman."

"That is not possible. I will remind you that you are not *our* commander. We listened too readily to your dangerous advice. You must now wait until we have made our decisions. Out."

Koenig shoved the handset back in its clip and flipped switches along the instrument spread to lift Car Thirty-nine out of the sea. He circled the tower. There was not much left to burn in the gaunt upper floors. Already the flames were less and would die of their own accord. The structure had taken a greater hammering in the past and had settled to a monolithic stability that would not be challenged now. All the loose material that was being shaken out was coming down on the seaward face from the angle of tilt. On the land side, there was no immediate danger. He took the car down and landed on the terrace.

It was clear that some auto sprinkler device had gone into action on the first floor. Halfway up the ramp, they met a thick tide of grey sludge. The first floor was ankle deep in globules of grey foam. The air was acrid with the stench of burning. It would be a long time before it was habitable again.

Helena said, "On Alpha we had deep shelters to use in emergency. That's where they'll be. They'll all have gone underground."

Rhoda said, "The dock area. There's nowhere else that I know about."

Koenig turned on his heel. There was no point in looking further in the living quarters. When they reached the massive concrete seal, it was shut. There was safety enough behind it. Only an atomic strike would breach that barrier. But it moved easily enough on its counterweights and gave them access to the long quay and the mute stranded freighter, which gave silent testimony to the long-gone aggro of another people in another time.

Even now, after all the years, the tiny remnant of the Megaronian people were still at it. There was another feature, as old as time. All along the quayside, the Outfarers' community was spread out in little family groups, with their bundles of belongings arranged around them to mark out a piece of territory in the confusion. It was a refugee camp.

Some had already settled down to sleep. Others were still standing about, unable to come to terms with the spin of the wheel that had brought their settled routine to a jarring full stop. They watched the Alphans pass. Bewilderment and hostility were equally evident, but they made no open move against them.

Farther on, as they turned into the strike-craft base, there was more evidence that hard decisions had been made and a new line taken. The defence corps was all present and under arms. But command of it had clearly passed to the bearded Golgos. Hung around with sidearms and carrying a machine pistol on a shoulder strap, he was conducting some kind of kangaroo court. Those being brought for trial were isolated in a group on the slipway, as though already part way out of the community home. Two men with machine pistols at the ready were on guard to keep them there. The rest were sitting or leaning on the gravity conveyor, listening to the new top hand.

There were five for the pogrom. Karl had his arm round Gelanor's shoulders and was doing his best to comfort her. Victor Bergman was leaning on the wall, arms folded, genial ape's face sombre and thoughtful. The other two were Hepa and Urion—the two councillors of the platform party who had voted for the Alphans and had, seemingly, refused to change their view.

As the Alphans came into earshot, they heard Golgos reach the key section of his address. ". . . .That emergency has arrived. I, therefore, invoke Clause Twenty of the Constitution. I declare that the Code is suspended for one month and that military law operates. That means that the defence corps itself is the council. Is that agreed?"

There was a chorus of assent. The only objection came from Karl, who left Gelanor and strode up the ramp, until he was stopped by the muzzle of a pistol against his chest. He said, "You have gone too far, Golgos. The Constitution also says that such a decision can only be taken by a full meeting of Outfarers. You are outside our law."

Whatever his expertise as a lawyer, Golgos could react smartly to a situation. As Karl spoke, he saw the Alphans and his pistol was swept round to aim at Helena Russell. He said, "Let them join their friends. We will deal with them all at once."

Carter's hand was on the butt of his laser. Koenig saw the move out of the tail of his eye. There was no doubt they could make Golgos pay; but there was no doubt, either, that they would end up dead. He said,

"Law is law in any community. We accept the need to live by it. What we were trying to do was in the Outfarers' long-term interest."

Another voice joined the dialogue. Melanion had been keeping himself off the centre of the stage, but he came forward. "*Tried,* you say. So all this is for nothing? We have lost our homes on a foolish gamble."

Before any of his party could speak, Koenig said, "Spadec was alerted. It was as though they knew there would be a visit to the farm. As we reached it, a big force arrived from Caster to guard it. We were lucky to escape. We did not expect congratulations, but at least we should expect credit for working on your behalf."

To his relief, there was no further pressure on that one. He had no wish that a signal should go to Caster saying that they had succeeded and that there had been some tampering with the food supplies. If that could be concealed, there was still a delayed-action psychological bomb planted in Caster, which might give the human spirit a new twist.

Helena Russell and Alan Carter caught his drift. Rhoda, who might have blurted out the truth, was hooked on a different train of thought. She was staring at Melanion, as though seeing him plain for the first time and not liking it. She said bitterly, "I don't understand you, Father. Why are you not with Gelanor and Karl? Why are you against my friends?"

"Your friends, as you call them, have come near to destroying us all. They should never have been accepted in this community. We had come to a balance with Caster. They did not interfere with us as long as we kept within these walls."

"They beat *me.* I still have the marks. Or had you not noticed? See!"

Rhoda ripped down the seals of her suit and peeled off the top half. Aggravated by sea and sand, her stripes were livid and angry.

Melanion said, "Have you no shame, girl? Cover yourself. There was no need for you to be taken. You are headstrong and disobedient. You were outside the prescribed limits. You brought it on yourself. That is no argument."

Golgos could see that the clear edges of decision were getting blurred. He said harshly, "All this takes us nowhere. The past is past. Move along before I lose all patience."

Koenig could read the harmonics. Golgos was a young man with a reputation to make. He might well push himself into a situation that could only be resolved by blood. Somebody had to lower the temperature. He said evenly, "The majority may be wrong. Nevertheless, it is always right. A community must come to its own decisions. I would only suggest that they are best not taken in haste or on the rebound from a disaster. Believe me, we understand how you must feel. But I would say this. What you have just suffered shows only too clearly that you hold your tenancy here on a thread. The council should think about that, when they plan for the future."

Before Golgos or Melanion could reply, he led off to the head of the slipway. The guards stood aside and the three Alphans together with Rhoda joined the party already assembled there.

Rhoda made a direct line for Gelanor. There was more than the political angle to worry her. She had a sudden, clear insight that she was emotionally committed to the Alphan captain. Her nerves were raw after the alarms and exertions of a long night and she was near to tears.

Gelanor put her arms round her daughter in a way she had not done since she was a small child. Looking over her shoulder, she could see Melanion staring down at them both, his thin face set and bitter.

Events had moved them all to a point of no return. Gelanor was making a private statement to ease her daughter's mind, where she could see there was a deep hurt. In so doing, she set herself on the wrong side of the law. But her voice was steady and carried the ring of truth. "Do not grieve about Melanion, Rhoda. You owe him no duty. He is not your father."

Melanion was hearing out loud something he had known for long enough in his mind. It made the fact no more palatable. For a moment, Koenig believed that he would snatch a machine pistol from the nearest guard and shoot both women where they stood. Karl had returned down the slipway to join the Alphans and was about to speak. Guessing what he would say, Koenig took his arm in a vise-like grip. "Save it, Karl. It will do no good."

Melanion had mastered his sudden rage and was going coldly to work in a different direction. All would be done by the due process of law. He said, "We waste time. Let us proceed. Golgos is right. The Constitution allows for martial law. This is an emergency and the people can not meet. The defence corps is the council. I now propose that Golgos, as leader of the defence corps, shall hold the office of dictator while the emergency lasts. Who is in favour?"

Assent was immediate and total. Military government had voted itself into power. Melanion said, "The first act of our leader must be to rid us of these traitors. I also invoke the ancient law against the woman Gelanor, who has broken the solemn undertaking of a twenty-year pairing contract."

Golgos could have well done without the complication. But the pairing code was central to the Outfarers' organisation. A small community, fighting for a toehold in hostile conditions, needed stability and could not afford the tensions of a sexual free-for-all. When a contract was made by a man and a woman, it was ratified by the council and was sacrosanct for a fixed term, however difficult the assenting parties found it. Within living memory, there had been no case of a breach brought to public declaration.

He needed advice and Melanion was there to give it. Plainly, he was all set to be the grey eminence, the power behind the throne, and the role would suit him.

Melanion said, "There is no need to take evidence.

The offence is admitted before all these witnesses. Sentence can be passed by the leader. It is death or banishment."

Karl shook himself free from Koenig and went to Gelanor and Rhoda. Arms round them both and, in a way, glad to have the right at last to do it openly, he said, "Then the sentence applies equally to me."

There was a stir in the ranks. Karl had been a popular figure and, except in the last difficult days, had commanded respect from all the community. Golgos was no fool and sensed that an extreme sentence might cause dissension. He thumped the hull of a strike craft with the butt of his pistol to get silence. He said, "We will follow the rule of law. I decree that Karl and Gelanor are to leave the enclave. They have one hour to collect what things they can carry. Beyond that time, they are declared outlaws and will be shot on sight. Is that agreed?"

There was not much enthusiasm for it, but the chorus of assent was positive enough. Golgos went on. "For the strangers, the case it different. They have broken no law, but they have shown that they are not suitable to be taken into our community. Even at first, there was doubt and the vote to accept them was divided. I reverse that decision. They must go. They also have one hour. Beyond that time, they will be hunted down, if they remain within ten kilometres of this place."

Under cover of the vote, which was by acclaim in this case, Victor Bergman looked sharply at Koenig. He said, "Is that deliberate, John? Is he leaving it open for a death penalty in any event? How do we get out of the proscribed area in that time?"

The same thought had occurred to Koenig. He said, "We have the means. It's a question of getting out without a guard detachment on our backs."

Golgos had one more piece of business. He said, "There remains the case against Hepa and Urion. These two councillors supported Karl and the Alphans against our interest. They lose all citizen privileges and revert to the lowest grade of manual work."

At a signal from Golgos, the guards at the head of the slipway backed off. The whole defence corps lined the quay, pistols aimed at the group below. For a moment, Koenig believed that the judicial procedure had been a charade and execution would follow anyway. But there was no other move except the silent threat. Time was moving on. He gathered his people and strode up the slope with Victor Bergman beside him. Helena and Carter followed, then Karl and Gelanor, with Rhoda between them. After a moment's hesitation, Hepa and Urion joined the column.

Knowing that flight invites pursuit, Koenig kept the pace unhurried until they were through the arch that took them out of sight and brought them to the main quay. Rhoda had not been mentioned on any capital charge. It might occur to Golgos for private reasons, and to Melanion from sheer spite, that she, at least, should be held back.

They were halfway along the dock when a warning shot whistled overhead and a detachment of guards came through the arch at the double. Koenig snapped out, "Get ahead, Alan. Have the slab ready to drop." To Karl he said, "Get them along. As fast as you like!"

The refugees were a cover. Random fire would drop more friends than outlaws. But the last twenty metres would be critical. Koenig whipped the rest on and took the rear with his laser set for a wide-angle stun beam. He saw Hepa and Urion with five metres to go for the hatch and caught up as they reached it. All hands heaved on the counterweighted slab and it was down for a full due as a volley slammed into its blank face.

Koenig heaved down the lever to activate the lock and blasted it with a laser beam that melted it to a stub. Golgos would have to send a detachment out through the strike-craft port to sort it out. But there could be other ways out of the complex. There was no time to hang about.

Outside, the sky was lighter. The long night had finally moved itself to a new dawn. The ruined tower had never looked attractive. Now it was a disaster area, scorched, drab and evil smelling. The small air car was fully laden with nine passengers and the litter of gear stripped from the wreck of Eagle Seven. She moved sluggishly for a lift-off. Koenig circled the building. Small fires still guttered at the high levels and a thin plume of black smoke was rising against the sky. A dawn wind was wrinkling the surface of the sea.

Helena said, "Where do we go now, John?"

Koenig followed the military maxim. Never show doubt. Any order is better than no order. Sound as if you had it all buttoned up and could see farther through the wood than the next man. He said, "For a first stop, there's only one place. Victor pointed it out on the map. There's a deserted space-programme site, as I understand it. We'll see if there's any accommodation we can use, until we sort something out."

The small car picked up a course and moved inland down the peninsula, away from Caster and the Outfarers both.

By the time the slab was lifted and Golgos had his defence corps questioning round the site, there was no trace of the quarry and nothing to show which way they might have gone.

CHAPTER SEVEN

In the dawn light, the central plateau of the small peninsula was stark and barren as a moonscape. Approaching the site on foot, it would have been difficult to build up an intelligent picture of the area, but from the air, they could see it whole. It had been a massive enterprise, a minor city in itself.

The remnants of a perimeter fence still stood, running in a circle on a diameter that must be all of two kilometres. Set back from the fence was a broad inner wheel, which had been set out in eight arcs for housing development, in squat single-storey blocks with circulation avenues leading to the centre. At the hub of the system was an oval outcrop of rock which had been machine trimmed to a smooth regular shape and lay like a long barrow or a stranded whale. Along its broad back, three immense circular covers lay like pan lids on a cooker.

Bergman, fairly bouncing on his seat, called the pilot. "Do you see that, John? Launching silos. Intercontinental ballistic vehicles. Or missiles? Is it a defence system?"

Karl answered him. "You understand, Professor, this is outside our experience; but what we have pieced together of our history says that it is neither of those things. We know that the Megaronians of the great cities had launched ships into space. This was one of the great centres of the space programme."

Koenig took them down to a perfect landing at the

end of an avenue, where a clear paved area surrounded the bank of silos. From ground level, the scale was suddenly enormous. They were midgets in a giant's playpen. Fully staffed, the base might well have been home and work place for twenty thousand people. They had it to themselves.

Koenig could not say what he had expected to find, but he knew for a truth that unless he got his party on load, the sheer, depressing weight of their surroundings would sap their will to move. He said, "First things first. We'll look around this sector. I'd like to get the car out of sight. Just in case Mestor gets a signal and takes it into his head to look for us. Then a roof over our heads."

Helena Russell, never far off his wavelength, said, "We have the medical kit from Eagle Seven. I can run tests on any water supply we find. But what about food, John? Rationed out, those emergency packs won't stretch much beyond a week for nine."

"Then we have a week to get something organised. Conference on that as soon as we're settled in. As of now, split up in twos and search about. Don't be too particular. It's a warm climate; we don't need anything fancy."

Helena Russell joined him and the others moved slowly away from the car. He could see the lines of strain on her fine-boned face. Wide-spaced eyes were enormous. He said, "I'm sorry, Helena. You must be tired out. It won't be long. Then we can catch up on some sleep."

"No more tired than you must be. You've had the extra strain of thinking ahead for us. I'm the doctor. I should be prescribing a rest for you. What do you really think, John? Can we make anything of this place?"

"There's no choice. Not in the short term. In the long term, who knows? There were life signs from other areas. Maybe they haven't all opted for the way of life in Caster. We have the car. Alan can check what range it gives us on the fuel that's left. There are endless possibilities. This is a very select party. We have a medico, a scientist who has a flair for improvisation and people who have made a life on this planet out of the rubble of one city. The life force, or whatever it is, that brought us this far, hasn't done with us yet."

Hands behind her back she said, "I suppose I needed a lecture. All right, let's go. Where do we look first? Mind you, I think I know what you'd like me to say. The others will find a house. We'll look at that launch silo or whatever it is."

They crossed the wide pavement hand in hand. When they were close, the natural-rock wall towered up like a smooth cliff. It was a tribute to human skill and ingenuity. The builders had found a natural landscape feature and adapted it for their purposes. Its immense mass would give thermal and acoustic insulation for even a rocket blasting out of a silo. It would be a radiation screen also. Koenig leaned both palms on the flat rock and said slowly, "When this civilisation ran out of steam and the war lords were saturating themselves and everybody else with nuclear fallout, a place like this would be as safe as a deep shelter. The last men here cleaned up and left it tidy. Men like Victor. What would they think?"

"That there was a long night coming, but that in the distant future the work might start again."

"Like a pharaoh, building his pyramid to outlast the millenia."

She could have reminded him that the elaborate tombs hardly lasted a decade before tomb robbers had bored their beetle way into the treasure vaults, but she kept it to herself. Enthusiasm was as good a stimulant as any drug in the pack. Disappointment was one thing, at least, that could wait until tomorrow.

They were about a third of the way along the long axis of the great hump of rock. They walked slowly to the nearer end, examining the side for some way of access. There was none.

Koenig said, "They'd need to get in there with

heavy servicing gear. Fuel, maintenance, supplies of all kinds. Maybe it all went by underground roadways. But from where?"

Round the corner, he found part of his answer, but they had to stand well back to see it plain. The scale was so vast that at close quarters the edges were lost. Fifty metres wide and twenty metres high, there was a single slab, textured to meld into the face, but showing a faint colour change that marked it out as a single unit.

Helena said, "There's your way in, John. But how in heaven's name do you open it?"

It was a good question. There were no easy answers to it. Koenig thought aloud. "It's like the keep of a motte and bailey castle. A last ditch home for the defenders. This one they fix so that there's no way in from outside. So it has to be opened from the inside. Because the people who were inside would not expect to stay inside forever."

"So we get inside and then we can let ourselves out? You've lost me."

"But what else did they have in a Norman keep?"

"A well? A dungeon? A bolt hole? That's what you're getting at. They had a bolt hole. If the day was finally lost, they could get out under the moat and come up behind the enemy. Is that what you mean?"

"Something like that. But I was thinking that you don't open a massive entrance like this one every time a crewman goes off duty. This isn't for personnel. Somewhere we'll find underground access for people."

"Sealed."

"Surely, sealed. But it has to be easier to tackle than this."

Back at the car, he took a round up of reports. The sector they were in had been a dormitory area. The buildings had been developed on a plan. Three blocks were subdivided into suites of rooms leading off a central corridor. Each unit had a lounge area, with a small food-preparation alcove, a washroom and two bedrooms. The fourth block of each set was for community use. It was divided into public rooms for dining and recreation. The ancient Megaronians had hit a nice balance for the public and private aspirations of those who lived permanently on the base.

What was surprising to each pair of searchers was the way the site had been left. There was no detritus of occupation, no clutter of broken and abandoned gear. The rooms had been systematically cleared out and left as empty shells. There was no glass in any window space, no door in any frame, but there was no rubble of broken shards or shattered woodwork. There was only dust, even and undisturbed on every horizontal surface.

Victor Bergman said, "It's amazing, John. It was an orderly and controlled shutdown. There's nothing useable to be found. But why go to that trouble if the base was abandoned in a crisis?"

Helena Russell said, "In a widespread social disaster, there'd be millions of dispossessed people looking for a place to live. If there was nothing here to attract them, they'd go elsewhere. Places like the one the Outfarers found would offer more. Perhaps that was the point? The organisers of the base took a long view. They didn't want it overrun. Given the framework intact, they believed they could revitalise it in another age when the troubles were over."

Koenig said, "That speaks of a long-term view, and it means that a cadre of top management was still in control and still on the site and, for that matter, still strong enough to carry out its will. Where did they get to?"

By a kind of group suggestion, all eyes tracked round to look at the monolithic *mastaba* in the centre of the base. It was giving away no secrets, but the clue to the enigma was there. Nothing short of a direct hit with an atomic warhead could breach its blank walls. There would be room inside to house an army.

Karl said, "You must understand that the time you are speaking of is so long gone that we have no rec-

ords of it. I believe that those who survived the great
upheavals were so incensed at the scientific knowledge
that had made it possible that they deliberately de-
stroyed all records that could be found."

Koenig said, "It can happen. A burning of the
books. Books are blamed rather than the use that people have made of them."

A quiet man, Urion had hardly spoken since he
was bundled into the car. Now he said, "Who can say
that it is not sometimes necessary? The weeds of evil
may thrive more tenaciously than the good seed.
When that happens, it may be prudent to burn the
whole field and plant afresh."

It was the definitive statement to end the dialogue.
Koenig kicked his jaded mind into action. "Where's
this mess hall? We'll run the car inside and break out
some rations. Then a spell of rest."

After the meal, Urion approached Koenig. "I expect, Commander, you will wish to have one member
of the party keeping watch. Allow me the privilege of
being first."

Hepa joined him. "You and I are the only ones who
had some sleep last night. It would be a lonely vigil. I
will watch with you."

Never one to discourage a volunteer, Koenig said,
"You are right. I had it in mind and I thank you."

There was not much comfort to be had. But at least
it was not cold. Already, there was warmth in the Sun.
They dragged squabs out of the car and made a mat-
tress for Helena and Rhoda. The others lay on
smooth, thermo-plastic tiling, with bundles of clean-
ing waste, from the car's maintenance locker, as a pillow. Koenig slept like a sailor as soon as his head
touched down.

Urion's hand was a centimetre from Koenig's
shoulder when the Alphan's eyes flicked open and his
fingers closed on the butt of his laser. The Outfarer
said, "You sleep lightly, Commander. I wish you

would have slept longer, but the time is up when you said I should wake you."

"You did right. Has anything happened?"

"Nothing, Commander. All is quiet. It is strange here. Both Hepa and I have felt the strangeness, as we sat quietly. It is as if the spirits of those who worked here so long ago were watching us. But as we sensed it, they were not hostile. Rather, they were curious, as though they wanted to know what we would do."

Koenig debated about whether to waken Helena. On balance, he decided he would have to do it. Her independent spirit would not accept favours, even from him. She would want to work the same stint as anybody else. Hepa settled down in her place and Urion composed himself with his arms crossed on his chest like a stone figure on a catafalque.

The two Alphans made a check of all the stores which had been transferred hurriedly from Eagle Seven. Koenig stripped open a flat pack, which he had judged was a self-inflating dinghy. In fact, it held ten, one-piece white coveralls. The dinghy might have made a bed, but this was even more useful for those still wearing the neoprene wet suits.

When they had changed, he brought out the Eagle communications panel and a maintenance kit from the car. Helena Russell said, "Is it worth trying to repair it? Who do we have to communicate with?"

"It has more range than the car. Who knows? We might hear from Main Mission."

"They can't help us."

"True. But I'd like to hear them."

"Could we speak to them?"

"Not by voice. Perhaps by a Morse signal."

Protective fuses had blown on every circuit. There were no spares. He untwisted a length of multicore lead and bypassed every safety point. It was rough work and any Eagle technician would have turned grey, but he reckoned it would hold up as a temporary repair. When it was done, he carried the panel into the car and searched the instrument spread for a power source.

Helena Russell squatted on her heels and watched him. For her, this was a new side to his character. She said, "I'm impressed. I didn't know you had such a practical flair. I thought top pilots didn't know what went on under the hood."

"I hope I shall always be able to surprise you."

"You'll really surprise me if Paul's voice comes out of that."

In the event, it was Sandra's meticulous tones that sounded very faintly into the car. They looked at each other in silence, each suddenly sidetracked by memories of Moonbase Alpha.

Sandra said, "Main Mission to Eagle Seven. Perhaps you can still receive our signal. We will continue to keep this link open as long as there is any remote chance that you could receive our signal. Life signs on the monitors tell us that you are still alive. We wish you good luck, if that can be."

The immense power of Alpha's transmitters could push a voice signal over the distance. There was no chance that the jury-rigged panel could match it. Koenig rapidly dismantled the handset and used bare contacts for a make and break. Taking it slowly, he spelled out: "Koenig calling Alpha. I read you. Over."

Even at strength one, there was no mistaking the excitement in Sandra Benes's voice. "Commander! We read you. Is there anything we can do?"

Koenig suddenly recognised that any transmission he made was a homing beacon for Caster's scout cars if they decided to search. He made it short. "We send our greetings. I will call again in two hours. Brief calls only. Out."

Helena's eyes were shining. She said, "It makes a difference. I don't feel so *isolated*."

"Eventually they will be out of range."

"I know that, but we know now that Alpha is operational again and they know we're still alive. I can't explain it, but I still feel better about it."

Carter and Rhoda took the next stint, then Bergman and Karl. At each watch change, there was a brief contact with the distant base. By mid-afternoon, the whole party was rested and ready for the next thing. They turned naturally to Koenig for a definition of what that would be. He said, "As I see it, the key to this complex is behind that rock. We have to find the way in. It isn't wasted time. While we do it we can check out the rest of the site for anything useful. We go together to the next sector, split and search each building, then we go on to the next in line. We're looking for access to a lower level."

They had the equipment belts from the wet suits, hung about with sidearms and the vibrators that Carter and Koenig had never discarded. Contact with Alpha had given the four Alphans a new surge of optimism. Rhoda had listened to Sandra's voice and was glad she was a world away. She had seen Alan Carter's pleasure and was choosing to put a feminine twist on it. As they walked off she said, "This Sandra with the cool voice. Is she very pretty?"

"Very pretty. You'd like her. Everybody likes Sandra."

"You work with her?"

"She's our data analyst. Top in the field."

"If she is so beautiful and so clever, you must be in love with her."

Carter suddenly saw the pit that had been dug for him. "Ah! Well, no. She had what you would call this pairing arrangement with Paul Morrow."

"So she rejected you. But you still love her."

Carter stopped, took her shoulders and turned her to face him. A simple man, he could only stick to fact as he saw it. He said, "I enjoyed living on Alpha with many good friends that I miss, but if it was a choice between Alpha without you and this crazy world of Megaron with you, I guess I should have to choose Megaron."

Gold-flecked eyes were serious and searching. Then her arms went impulsively round his neck. When they caught up with the column, Koenig and Helena were already searching the first block in the new sector.

It was the first of many and Koenig was driven to the conclusion that all the building on the side they were on was for accommodation. The parallel of the castle was keeping up. The courtyard was for housing the workers. The high command had its place in the tower.

They missed out a number of sectors and rounded the far end of the central rock. There was evidence here also of a huge slab entrance for major equipment. A wide roadway ran straight to the perimeter. On either side, the buildings were long, empty storage sheds. They marked a change in the building plan. The next sector was clearly not for accommodation and might well have been an admin silo. Floors still showed traces of discolouration where hardware had been bolted down.

Victor Bergman said, "This looks very like an operations centre, John. They'd administer the outer zone from this point. Flow control for stores coming in. All the thousand and one details to keep tabs on personnel. A kind of city hall."

Helena Russell had been examining an interior wall. She called, "John!" and the excitement in her voice had the whole party turning to watch her. Palms flat on a slightly corrugated surface, she was lifting a flexible shutter which retracted into a housing in the ceiling.

When it was away for a full due, they stood in a line looking into five elevator cages with dull, bronze gates. Four were closed, intact and undisturbed. The centre one had its gate forced from its hinges and leaned against the back wall. The centre of the floor had been broken through in a ragged opening almost a metre across.

It was the first evidence that others had visited the

site after the careful shutdown. Tomb robbers had been at work.

A sound crossed Koenig's audio threshold and he knew it had been building up for some time before he recognised it. Rhoda was on to it at the same time. She said, "An air car!"

Koenig said, "Get down. Below window level."

The hum built to a drone and a racing shadow flicked across the floor. The pilot was flying low, taking a look along the radial avenues.

Lying next to Koenig, Karl said, "If he's observant, he might see traces of where we first landed."

Koenig said, "It's a long chance, but we can't ignore it." He moved to the open door and looked out. The car had run on to the perimeter and was turning. It flew back the way it had come and went out of sight behind the rock.

Hepa said bitterly, "Even here they are hunting us. They are not content even to let us die in our own time."

With an arm round her shoulders, Urion comforted her, "Have courage. It may not come to that. And nobody knows we have come here. Now that they have looked here and not found us, they will look elsewhere."

Koenig went back to the elevator trunk. Leaning well into the hole, he shone a light down the shaft. Counterweights hung in a channel in the rear wall. Another channel held a broad metal strip perforated with foot- and handholds. It would be possible to hang below the cage on a crossbeam, traverse hand over hand and reach it. He pulled back and explained what he had seen to Bergman.

"I know you, John. You won't rest until you've taken a look. Perhaps we should bring the car here and make this our base?"

"I want progress. I'm not satisfied that the car has a nil report. He'll be in Caster in fifteen minutes. We could have them on our backs again in under the hour. This is the best hideaway we've seen yet. But you have a point." He turned to Alan Carter. "Alan. You and Karl get to the car. Load the gear and bring it along. Meantime, we'll take a look below. All right?"

"Check, Commander."

"And watch how you go. Just in case that car dropped a foot patrol before we saw it."

"I'll do that."

Koenig fixed his lamp on a headband and dropped below the cage. Bergman took his place on the floor and watched him move easily across to the ladder. As Koenig's feet touched the footholds he saw the band shiver and a warning was stillborn in his throat as Koenig's weight went fully onto it. There was no time to get it out. The Alphan was already slipping away. The band was free to move.

But it was friction loaded. He was going down steadily, but with no acceleration. On a count of ten, the band shivered to a stop and Koenig was looking up the well. "Victor."

"Yes, John."

"There's a big landing and a corridor going towards the rock. This was the way in for personnel. . . . And, Victor. . . ."

"Yes?"

"No worry about getting back. There's a locking lever here for the band."

The light disappeared as he left the bottom of the shaft. Victor Bergman sat back on his heels, his genial ape's face creased in sudden thought. There was something that did not jell and he was a good minute before he knew what it was. He put it to Helena. "Here's a logical puzzle. This ladder moved down with John's weight. He says he can fix it solid to climb up. Now, we believe that somebody opened the floor and went down there. How did they climb out?"

"You've just told me. They fixed the ladder so that it was not free to move."

"But just now, when we found it, it was free to move. Who released the lever down below?"

"The last man."

"And how did he get out?"

Rhoda had been watching the exchange, looking from one to the other. She said, "Unless he used a rope or another ladder, he's still down there."

As if on cue, Koenig's voice reverberated up the shaft. "Helena!"

She leaned into the hole in the floor, presenting him with a disembodied head.

"John?"

"Your tomb robber. He didn't get very far. He's still here."

"How did he die?"

"Violently."

"I'll come down."

She fixed her headband lamp and made a neat, athletic job of swinging along to the ladder. With more light, it was easier to see the layout. The corridor from the circular landing area was ten metres wide and three metres high. It had once been lit by a continuous lighting strip recessed in the roof. The floor was tessellated with blue and yellow tiles under a thin screen of dust. It led straight as a die to a red corrugated shutter which closed off the far end. Footprints in the dust showed the pattern of Koenig's sneakers forward and back. One other set, fainter and dusted over, had a one-way ticket.

Their owner was lying face down, a metre from the shutter, skeletal hands fixed to the sides of his skull, legs drawn up, miming the last human gesture he had made. Something had struck silently and unexpectedly and brought his journey to a full stop.

Koenig said, "Not too close. Whatever he ran into might still be operational. I'd say he tripped some relay and triggered a protective force field."

He looked more closely at the footsteps. They went on to a point beyond where the feet were lying. The killing blow had come at a point somewhere along the site of the corpse. He went forward, half a step at a time, dropped to a full knee bend, keeping his head back, and took hold of the bony ankles. There was so little weight, that he almost fell back. Then he was out of the danger zone, drawing his hollow man after him.

Clothing showed no sign of decay. He was wearing thonged sandals, a fluted metal cloth tabard of silver grey, belted at the waist, and an embroidered *chiton* almost knee length. Hidden by the body and dragged along with it was a curious, bulbous-nosed handgun.

No stranger to death, Helena Russell shivered. There was something lonely and sad about the dead Megaronian. He had lain there for many centuries, with his violent end unmarked by any rites of passage. After the breakup of the great cities, there would have been many lonely, wandering men and women ending their days in bitterness and isolation. It was, anyway, more than likely to happen to the Alphans themselves, and this was a preview.

She said, "I think you must be right. Death was sudden and he had no way of avoiding it. Perhaps it was an automatic device or, perhaps, at that time, the rock was still held and this was a deliberate, selective strike."

Koenig shone his light slowly over the roof. The tiled roof was solid and showed no opening which might house a beam system. There was a call down the shaft and Helena went to check it out. It was Victor Bergman. "Tell John that Alan's back. No trouble. As far as he can tell, there was no patrol left behind."

Koenig joined her. "I heard that. I'd like you and Alan and Karl down here. What can we use to make a scaffold?"

"Three of the squabs?"

"Right. As soon as you like. Tell the others to keep their ears open. If Mestor sends a mopping-up party, we can hold out down here. They can pass the gear down."

With Carter and Karl steadying two uprights and a seat squab lying across the top, Koenig had a working platform. He used a vibrator to slice out a panel in the lighting strip and then moved slowly along. The duct contained short lengths of tube filled with a blue gas. Every other one, had an angled camera-type fitting beside it.

Bergman said, "They monitored this passage pretty thoroughly. Nobody would get along here without being seen."

As they reached the site of the long-gone execution, he broke out a strip running to the end of the footsteps. There was a new feature. A fan-shaped fitting of bright metal filled the lighting trough. An emission from it would cover the corridor wall to wall. Using his laser and standing back, he sent a searing beam at the inlet and where it appeared at ceiling level. The whole structure glowed and finally began to deform. Finally it broke free and dropped clear.

At the same moment of time the whole lighting strip glowed into brilliant life, and Urion called urgently down the shaft: "Commander! There is a squadron of air cars circling the complex."

CHAPTER EIGHT

Koenig weighed up the options. The Megaronians were determined to hound them. A last stand on the surface might make them pay dearly for it, but it could only end one way. On balance, they were better to dig in where they were. He organised the movement of as much of their stores as they could handle and then gathered his party in the vault.

He posted Carter at the bottom of the shaft. The first Megaronian to poke his head through the gap in the floor would have it ventilated by a terminal hole. Even if they went to work methodically and breached all the elevator cages, so that more than one at a time could drop to the lower level, the advantage still lay with the defence. Meanwhile, the only possibility of progress was to get inside the rock fortress. First priority was to see whether he had scotched the protective-beam gear.

A movement caught his eye. Urion had been talking to Helena and now knew the score. Before anybody could stop him, he walked firmly down the corridor, past the rickety dolmen of seat squabs and on towards the end.

Koenig's shout of "Wait!" went unnoticed or unheard. Urion had closed his mind to any outside interference. He reached the closed end still erect and unharmed and turned round to face them. He said simply, "It is safe."

Hepa was first to join him. She said, "That was very brave. You might have been killed."

He said, "I am nearest to oblivion of our party. I can most easily be spared."

"Not by me."

"I am old."

"What has age to do with it, when minds are in tune?"

Almost shyly he took her hand and kissed it. "You are very kind to say that."

Koenig and Karl joined them. Koenig said, "We are all grateful. Now we have to open this door. The engineers who devised it were contemporaries of those who built the city block. They might have used the same techniques. Search the walls and the floor for release gear."

Helena Russell found it, shoulder high in the right-hand wall; a section of tiling pivoted away to reveal a recess. Inside were the familiar levers.

Palms flat on the shutter, Koenig, Karl, Helena and Bergman heaved away and felt it lift. It was waist high when Koenig suddenly thought that there could be other protective gimmickry behind it. He said, "Hold it there!" and dropped to his knees to look through the gap. The interior was well lit, with no visible light source. Surfaces were dust free, clean and shining. Walls, floor and ceiling were clinically white. Directly ahead and twenty metres off, a flight of wide shallow stairs with bronze handrails ran up to the next floor. Craning his neck to follow them, he saw feet on the top landing and then the whole person of an incredibly ancient man in a blue, belted robe.

The advantage in the encounter was all with the oldster. He also knew who the visitor was, crouched on hands and knees at the foot of the throne. His voice was hardly more than a wheeze, but it carried the distance. "Commander Koenig. You may bring your people in. I shall not harm you."

Koenig was on his feet, laser in hand. There had been enough surprises on Megaron. He said, harshly,

"Your protective ray would have been all you needed. Why this change of heart?"

"I switched it off when I gave you light."

It could have been true. Koenig kept his eyes on the oldster and spoke to Bergman. "Take it up, Victor."

The slab at his back slid away into its housing. The old man spoke again. "I welcome you, Alphans and Outfarers. I am Cydon, the last custodian of the old wisdom. With me, the light goes out in Megaron."

It was a big claim to make, and before Koenig could comment on it, there was a further complication. Carter called urgently down the corridor, "Visitors, Commander!"

Cydon said, "You have no choice, Commander. You will have to trust me. Bring your people inside and close the seal. This time it will not open so easily, I promise you."

Koenig came to a decision. Cydon's offer, good or bad, had to be better than a slow war of attrition which could only end one way. He said, "Rhoda, tell Alan to fall back. Helena, pick up your medical kit. They can have the rest of the stores. I have a feeling we won't be needing them."

As the three rejoined the main body, a sustained burst of fire thumped down the well shaft. All turned to look. The great shutter began to drop from the ceiling, cutting off sight and sound. As it hit floor level, there was a definitive click and a subterranean rumble. The counterweight system had been disconnected. There was no way in for the attackers. And no way out for the besieged. Koenig spun on his heel. The stairway was empty. Cydon's wheeze came from nowhere in particular. "Do not be concerned. I was never with you. Come forward. You will have no difficulty in finding me."

Victor Bergman said, "Projection? That's feasible. A 3-D freestanding projection. This is very interesting, John. At last we might get to see how far the Megaronians went with their technology."

Cydon was the soul of truth in one thing at least. There was no problem in finding him. At the head of the stairway, there was an oval landing with a circular kiosk where a commissionaire might once have sat. Six corridors opened off. Only one was lit. They followed it to another oval interchange and on through another lighted corridor. At the end, there was an elevator with its hatch open, waiting to receive them. It took them up for a short, swift ride and stopped at a landing, where the character of the set showed a change. It was executive country: deep-pile carpets and walls panelled in light-yellow wood like pine.

A section of panelling slid silently aside. Cydon, if this was the real man and not another trick image, was standing on a strip of blue carpet, in a room that was partly furnished as a lounge area and partly fitted out with very sophisticated hardware. He was as tall as Koenig, thin to the point of emaciation, eyes deep sunk in a time-ravaged face. The eyes, like Rhoda's, were golden brown and contained all the vitality that the years had left him. He said, as though each word was fought over, "Be seated. You are not strangers to me. I watched from the moment you left your base on Earth's moon. It is a great pleasure to speak again at last. I have not spoken since Helice died. That must be twenty years ago."

Koenig could not help the thought that if the silence had been broken a little earlier, they would have been saved a lot of grief. He asked, "Do you have the power to speak to Alpha?"

"Indeed I do. This base was the nerve centre of our space programme."

"You did not think we would have welcomed a reply to our signals?"

Cydon might have been old, but he was far from stupid. He understood the criticism behind it. He looked round the circle before answering. When he did, it was obliquely. "You Alphans are a young and vigorous people. The civilisation of Megaron was old when your ancestors turned from a nomadic way of life to that of small, settled communities. There are great differences between us."

Helena said, "But, finally, you decided to help us. You could have left us to die outside your barrier. We thank you for allowing us to come through."

Cydon gave a long sigh. The strain of making personal contacts after his long solitude was beginning to tell. His voice was barely audible as he said, "There is much to discuss with you and I have very little time. We have watched the people of Caster for many years. It is time they awoke from their long sleep. Do not judge them too harshly. What was done there went wrong, but the intention was not bad in itself. You cannot understand the great trauma which the human spirit suffered on Megaron. Those who set up the system were protecting the community from the unfettered excesses of the human will, which had almost ended life on Megaron. In so doing, they stifled the striving and the good, which also exist."

Karl said, "I have seen more of the evil than the good."

"Just so. Just so. . . . But I must speak, while I can, to the Alphans. Perhaps I can help you. Look."

The old man, hardly more than a skeletal frame held together by the force of his mind, walked slowly to an instrument spread. On arrival, he leaned both hands on the console and gathered himself for the next move. Helena Russell, with a medico's interest, was half out of her chair to go to him, but he said, without turning round, "Thank you, Doctor Russell, but there is nothing you can do for me."

In the centre of the lounge area, there was a circular feature of blue tiling, like a large, empty plinth waiting for a statue. It began to fill from edge to edge with a swirling blue cloud. It grew thicker and more intense and then abruptly cleared, leaving in its place a 3-D miniature of the space base.

Tiny air cars drawn up on the terrace round the rock showed that the Megaronians had come in strength to hound the fugitives. Men were posted all round the admin silo.

The outer areas began to peel away as Cydon zoomed for a closer scan. They saw their own abandoned car and the head of the elevator shaft. Men were climbing down, carrying shoulder packs of what looked like blowtorch gear. Victor Bergman said, "Will they be able to break the seal?"

Still busy and changing the picture, Cydon said, "No. All the barriers are lined with infrangom. It is a metal which would interest you, Professor. Under pressure or in thermal agitation it gains greater strength. They have nothing which can penetrate it."

The scene had moved to the interior of the rock. They were seeing the inside of a spherical bunker with launch and guidance systems that were familiar enough to the four Alphans. A hatch opened and they looked along a connecting corridor to a second hatch which opened like an iris eye to let them through to a gantry. It dissolved to a long shot from a high point down an immense well, ringed every few metres by gantries and spidery stairways. In the centre, the whold space was taken up by a long, slender rocket ship.

Cydon slowly panned down her length. Silver cone, brilliant white superstructure, immense hydraulic jacks, red and black propulsion units. At the waist, there was s stylised emblem, a great, golden bird rising from tongues of vermilion flame. Below it was the motto: "wisdom shall rise again."

Carter said, "Holy cow. I thought our Ultra Probe was the last thing in spacers. *That* is a spacer. Did she ever fly?"

Cydon said, *"Phoenix* is a new ship. Her prototypes successfully probed to the nearer stars. She incorporates all the best features of her predecessors, with some refinements. She would fly. Of that there is no doubt."

Carter said bitterly, "We are just a few millenia

late for the passage. She only needs fuel and a back-up team. Little things like that."

Cydon went off at a tangent, his voice gaining a little strength as he spoke with pride of the past. "Three hundred of the elite corps of scientists and technicians sealed themselves away in this sanctuary when the world of Megaron went mad in an orgy of destruction. The secret of survival is energy. Energy is life. Food, heat, light, power. That we could organise, though we were cut off from the tidal generators which once supplied the base."

Bergman queried, "Reactors?"

"Not reactors, nor solar energy, though either would have been technically possible. No, the brief was to organise a simple, inexhaustible supply with no complications. The answer lies in the residual heat of the planet itself. Geothermal energy. A deep shaft was sunk. A heat exchange system using liquified gas was set up and is working to this day. There is no reason why you should not live out your lives here and other generations after you."

The human angle interested Helena. She asked gently, "And the others? Finally, you are alone."

"Ah, yes. . . . You must understand, we are speaking of many, many centuries. We endured here longer than most civilisations take to rise and flower and fall again. Looking back over that history, I believe that at some point a psychic weariness must have blunted the life force. The waiting was too long. Even hope does not endure forever. Fertility levels dropped. The community ceased to replace itself. Helice and I, the last pair to remain, had no children."

For Koenig, it was a preview of what could happen to Moonbase Alpha. Even the number of personnel was much the same. The human spirit needed space and freedom to grow. There was an idea in his mind which he hardly dared give house room, but he had to broach it. "Would the power from the geothermal well be enough to service *Phoenix* and launch her?"

"No."

Victor Bergman leaned forward in his chair and asked, "Is there fuel for her?"

"There is fuel. But the power needed to open the silo and activate the control gear is much beyond what I can command."

Carter said, "Is there no way?"

The question hung about unanswered. Cydon leaned heavily on his stick, as though he had already said too much and was regretting it. Then he lifted his head and looked at Koenig. "There is a way. Whether it could be done or not is another matter. I know what is in your mind and I will not try to prevent you. Why should I? I, too, would like to see *Phoenix* rise from Megaron as one last gesture from her days of greatness and perhaps, even, as a symbol of regeneration. The tidal generators supply the town of Caster with power. There is switchgear, which could divert that supply for us here. It would be dangerous and difficult and you are few to undertake such an enterprise. As in all matters of real importance, there is a choice. You have reached a certain sanctuary. Here you can live a comfortable life. That way, you would put all at hazard for the single chance of venturing again into the unknown."

Koenig considered it. All eyes were looking his way. He said slowly, "How is *Phoenix* manned? What numbers is she designed to carry?"

She is designed for a crew of six. But the key desks on the command island are only four. Navigation, power, communication and command."

Urion said, "I would not leave Megaron. If it will help you in your decision, Commander, do not consider me."

Hepa said, quickly, "Nor I. Even if it is possible— and how can that be?—I would stay with Urion."

Gelanor, glad to be able, at last, to be open about it, was holding Karl's hand. She said, "You have no problems on that score, Commander. Who knows what the future is for the Outfarers and for Caster? We may yet live to see a change and the beginning of a new way of life. We have fought too long for it to leave now. Am I not right, Karl? We shall stay?"

"Indeed, you are right." Karl covered her hand with his own.

Rhoda was very still, saying nothing. For once, she seemed to be out of programme. There was a moment's pause and Bergman filled the silence. "No contest, John. If we can launch *Phoenix,* we must go."

Helena Russell said, "I know you, John. You could never live with yourself if you missed a chance to reach Alpha. We have to try."

There was a small flurry of activity. Rhoda had jumped from her chair and was away out of the lounge area at a run. Alan Carter caught her in the corridor and she struggled to break out of his grip. When he turned her to face him, he saw that her eyes were full of tears.

"What is it? What's got into you, then?"

"Oh, you! How can you ask that?"

"What have I done?"

"Nothing."

"That's no answer."

His grip was too strong to break, but she could thump his chest and she did that, until he smothered the action.

Golden eyes blazing, she said, "I suppose I am not clever enough for your Moonbase Alpha? If you were all that clever, you wouldn't have got yourselves wandering the universe on a cinder heap!"

"Don't you want to come with us?"

"I have not been asked."

"Commander Koenig will give you a place on the ship."

"Commander Koenig! Commander Koenig! I don't care about your commander. I wouldn't be going for him."

The light dawned slowly on Alan Carter. A simple man of action, he had not thought that his position could be in any doubt. But she wanted it in clear terms. He bent down and swept her feet off the floor.

He said, "As for you, Rhoda, you have no choice. I *have* to go. Either you come quietly, or I'll shanghai you. I can't leave half my life on this rock."

"Shanghai? What sort of a word is that?"

"Shanghai, abduct, carry away, anything like that."

"You want me to go?"

"I love you."

"Well why didn't you say that in the first place?"

"I thought it was obvious."

"Let me down, then."

"Will you come?"

"Of course."

They walked back into the seminar, hand in hand.

Koenig had hardly noticed that they had gone. Suddenly there was a change in the whole situation, a U-turn which brought in so many new factors that his personal computer was racing to process the data. He had accepted Megaron as the butt and seamark of his utmost sail. Now there was a new horizon. Totally committed to the challenge, he paced Cydon's thick pile carpet. Once more, Moonbase Alpha was in the equation, and he knew that a stern chase was a long chase. Every minute on the clock took Earth's moon farther and deeper into the interstellar spaces.

He stopped. Facing Cydon, he asked, "What is your estimate of the time it will take to prepare *Phoenix* for countdown?"

"When I was a young man, I was given instruction in the launch procedures. It was a long time ago. All the information you need is to be found in the control bunker at the silo. Fuelling alone, as I remember, takes a full twenty-four hours. But while that is going on, you can familiarise yourself with the other details."

"Will local power sources be enough for that?"

"I believe so."

"Then we should start right away."

"I will direct you to the control bunker. You must excuse me if I stay here, but I will be available to give any help that is in my power."

"Do you have any idea of how we can reach the switchgear for the tidal generators?"

"That is easy to say, but it will be far from easy to carry out. I do not even know whether the supply cable is still intact and, indeed, whether it can still be followed. But it runs in a deep conduit across the peninsula. There will be a power control centre below Caster. It is, you might say, the reason why the town was sited in that place. Detailed plans are available. It was always known that we would have to make the reconnection, if *Phoenix* should be launched. At one time there was an annual inspection. But not in my lifetime."

Koenig recognised that a number of things must be done at the same time and he did not have the personnel to do it. The key to the operation lay at the power terminal. If he failed there, *Phoenix* would stay forever in her pit. That had to be right. In delegating jobs, one specialist picked himself. Victor Bergman was the only Alphan with the mathematical background to sort out the unfamiliar data of the Megaronian control systems.

He said, "Victor. Mission control falls to you. As soon as you like, get the fuel flowing in. Then run through prelaunch checks. I'd like Alan to be getting the feel of the navigation desk, but I can't spare him. For you and me, Alan, it's the long walk. We'll start as soon as we've had a quick look at the ship."

Carter said, "Check, Commander."

Karl had been listening intently to the exchange, and after a quick look at Gelanor, said, "Commander. You do not know what problems you might meet. Another man at your back could be important. Allow me to come with you. I think I know where we are heading and there will be duty guards at the power centre."

It was no time to refuse help. Koenig said, "I know you, Karl, and there's nobody I would rather have on a mission. Thank you."

To Cydon he said, "There's one more thing. You

said you could raise Alpha. I'd like to speak with the operations room there."

Cydon inclined his head and walked slowly to a long, elaborate communications spread. His bony fingers flipped switches in a row and a large screen glowed with silver rain. As it cleared, a gaunt sphere filled the frame, pockmarked with craters and lava dykes. The Alphans had seen it often enough below the jacks of their hurrying Eagles. Helena said, "Our moon!"

It was no paradise to offer to an impressionable girl and Carter said defensively, "Think of it as a spacer in mid-passage. Moonbase Alpha is comfortable enough."

Rhoda said, "Are you afraid that I can't stand a few problems. The place is unimportant, if you like the company you are with."

Sandra Benes's patient voice sounded over. "This is Main Mission calling Commander Koenig. We think you are still within range. Come in Commander Koenig."

Cydon beckoned and Koenig joined him. The Megaronian was tuning for magnification and the edges of the still were peeling away as the probes bore in. There was the silver glint of the domes and corridors of the sprawling base and then a last spurt, as though they had broken through the roof of Main Mission. The command island was there, with Sandra Benes looking at the big screen, dark eyes wide and incredulous as she stared at Koenig's hawk face looking down at her.

They heard her quick intake of breath. She said, "Paul! Kano! It's the commander!"

Koenig said, "It's good to see you. We have a race on, against the clock. There's an outside chance that we might get a spacer off the ground and catch up. Victor needs technical help. Keep the link open and have computer keyed in on remote."

Paul Morrow said, "Check, Commander. Can we meet you?"

"That might be necessary. But there's a whole lot of maybe in the equation. We'll keep in touch."

Cydon blanked the screen. He said, "We must conserve power where we can. You will be able to communicate from the control bunker or from the command cabin of *Phoenix*."

Rhoda said, "I like your people, Alan. Particularly the fair one who spoke. What is he called? Paul, did you say?"

"You don't think I'm going to let you talk to people, do you? You'll be locked in my cabin and only allowed out under my personal direction. Very likely on a short length of silver chain."

Cydon moved slowly and positioned himself deep in the recess of a horseshoe console. He said, "You are anxious to make a start, Commander. I can no longer make the journey into the silo. But I will lead you."

For a moment, Koenig believed that senility had won the day and that perhaps the whole of Cydon's offer had come from an unhinged mind. Then the old man was bathed in a shaft of brilliant light. When his voice came again, it was from an archway almost opposite to the one through which they had entered. All eyes tracked from the illuminated man to his *doppelgänger*, which stood in the arch, looking the more solid of the two.

"This way, my friends. After all these years, the plan of the sanctuary is as vivid to my mind as the palm of my own hand."

Certainly, there was no hesitation as Cydon projected himself through a maze of corridors, moving firmly at a good pace. Rounding a long, circular gallery, he explained, "There are three silos. *Phoenix* is in the centre one. We are passing the first. The ship here is unfinished. She is a small military craft, started when the intercontinental conflict became inevitable."

Koenig said, "And the third silo?"

"A missile. Against the wishes of the scientists, the government of the day insisted that the facilities of the base should be used for the war effort. Launching it would have brought swift reprisal. The people here contrived to delay, until the government was swept aside in the public upheaval. It was disarmed and made safe."

At the centre silo, Cydon stopped and indicated a massive hatch, sealed by wheel gear. He said, "Through there, you will be in more familiar territory than I am. I shall be ready to answer any questions you may ask." One second, he was there in full flower; the next, he was gone and they were alone.

Koenig spun the release wheels; a motor whined on load and slowly opened the hatch, which was a full metre thick. They stepped over the coaming to a gantry and the immense scale of the undertaking silenced all hands.

They had seen *Phoenix* scaled down, as a model to wonder at, in Cydon's lounge. Seeing her at close quarters, brilliantly lit along her shining length, she was a triumph of the human mind. Untold years of evolution had produced the race which had produced this marvel to carry them to the stars.

Both hands on the rail, Koenig looked up and down the sleek hull. He said, "Let no one say that man is insignificant. One way or another, he will make his mark and the universe will have to reckon with him."

Helena Russell said, "They could do this and yet they could not work out their personal relationships. Why is that?"

It was the ultimate question. Victor Bergman, from bitter experience, could say, "And not only here, Helena. Earth Planet has the same unbelievable problem. Science is ahead of the techniques of government. When we build the new Alpha, we shall have to do more to keep them in phase."

They clattered down a spiral staircase to a lower gantry and found the entrance to the control bunker. It was, as Cydon had said, a straightforward layout. Victor Bergman, excited as a schoolboy, went from console to console, identifying control systems and already making racing calculations on how they could be manned.

Controls were labelled in a language which was not familiar to the Outfarers; but, in addition, there was a pictograph system, which was plain enough to an experienced space scientist. He settled himself at the command desk and after a concentrated scan, picked out the start sequence for the fuelling system.

As though inspired by the spirit of the long-gone Megaronian controller, he went along the instrument spread, selecting switches. From the depths of the silo, there was the hum of machinery starting up. A stylised flow chart glowed on a monitor. They were in business. *Phoenix* was taking a transfusion of life blood.

Koenig left him to it. He and Carter dropped down two more gantries to reach the waist. Opening below the brilliant flames of the ship's emblem, the main hatch was reached by a broad ramp that lipped into the reception area. A central trunk with a hoist ladder, that could be a walkway when the ship was in flight, led to all sectors.

She was built in modules: a power pack with its control cabin; a well-found ward room; the command cabin with four desks on a command island; a dormitory module; a hydroponic tank section; and a communications outpost in the cone. The problems of space flight were the problems of space flight for any people at any time and the Megaronian designers had come up with solutions that both the Alphans had seen before. But there was no doubt about the quality of the craft. She was a superb piece of engineering.

Koenig said, "What do you think, Captain?"

"She'll go and we can fly her, Commander."

"So all we have to do is open the gate."

"That's all."

"Let's do that thing, then."

CHAPTER NINE

Helena Russell knelt by the manhold and watched Koenig's disappearing head like an Eskimo by a fishing hold and feeling as numb. The undertaking swayed between the extreme poles of being too easy and too hard. Against all rational hope, they had been given a second chance. Watching Victor Bergman, working like a living extension of the hardware, and looking at the sheer splendour of *Phoenix,* she could believe that the fantastic was no more than sober fact. But it all hinged on the human factors of three men, with all the odds against them.

She called down, "John!"

He stopped his downward climb and looked up, seeing her head circled in an aureole of light. "What is it?"

"Take care."

"I'll take care."

"Look. It's important, but it isn't the end of the world. I'd rather live here with you, than reach Alpha without you."

"Believe it, we'll reach Alpha, you and I, both."

"Good luck."

The shaft led to a sub-station, lit by a ceiling port, with flow diagrams on the walls and a control desk for two operators. Koenig checked round. It was plain enough. Once the cable was live, power could be channelled to the opening gear for the silo.

Carter found the hatch for the cable conduit and

he and Karl heaved it open. A metre below the coaming, the massive conductor went away into darkness, a black snake in a black pit. Hanging from the roof of the tunnel, hooked by pulleys to a monorail, was a flat tray with a seesaw lever mounted on a central pivot. Carter stepped onto it and gave an experimental push to the bar. He was two metres off and picking up speed, before he realised what he had found.

Karl said, "It's a maintenance trolley, commander. They'd send a crew along to inspect the cable. I've seen them before in the tunnels. It's going to make a lot of difference to the time."

It had been designed for two operators. The third man had every chance of being minced by the moving parts, but it was still a whole lot better than balance walking along the top of the cable. Carter and Karl stood at either end, pumping the lever, and Koenig stood on a handsbreadth ledge of clear deck, hanging on to a crossbeam between the two support stanchions.

The tunnel was dust dry and their passage raised a swirling grey mist behind them. Ahead, the view was always the same: as far as the beams of their lamps could go, there was grey, gunmetal cladding curving down to the endless ribbon of black cable. From visual clues, they could have been standing still below the same metre of monorail. But Carter's white coverall, blackened with sweat, was a silent testimony to the power he was putting into the pumping handle.

After a half hour, Koenig called a halt and shifted over to take Karl's place. The Megaronian said, "How far have we come, Commander?"

"It's hard to judge distances. Perhaps a third of the way."

They went on, falling into a tireless rhythm, a foretaste of limbo and the journey to the underworld. Karl relieved Carter at the leading end. It was hypnotic, mind bending. For Koenig's money, they could have been anywhere, leagues under the sea or a branch line circling the equator. When the character of the tunnel changed, he was slow to react, and they had gone a hundred metres into a white, tiled section on a gradual upward slope before he called, "Karl. Hold it!" and brought the swaying trolley to a halt.

They dropped to the top of the cable, glad to be moving on their own feet. After the draught of their passage, the air seemed stifling and hot. Up ahead, the slope levelled again and the tunnel opened into an oblong chamber. The cable humped, lifting itself in a curve. It disappeared into the roof for ten metres, then reappeared, to plunge on into the ongoing conduit. Whether it was the one they were looking for or not, they had gotten to a take-off point. Overhead was some kind of district sub-station. A line of rungs, set in the left-hand wall, led to a circular trap.

Three beams of light centred on it as they looked up. Alan Carter, voice hardly more than a breath, said, "If there's a duty detail up there, the first man through the hole will have to be quick."

There was nothing to be gained by looking at it. Koenig mounted the ladder. The underside of the hatch had a plain rim, with no evidence that there was any locking mechanism. The hinge was set on the wall side. It was simply a plug to keep out the draughts and stop any absentminded engineer from falling through with his cocoa.

He tried to visualise the room above. Very likely, any load-bearing wall would be set directly above the wall below, so the hatch would open against it. He looked at the cable. That would feed directly to the control panels. An operator sitting there would either be facing him over the desk or have his back to him. It was a fifty-fifty chance.

He went up another rung, flattened his palms on the underside of the lid and pushed. There was resistance and then he felt it move a centimetre. Slowly, he settled it back. He said, "Up beside me, Alan. They can only be surprised once."

As Carter climbed up, Koenig took his laser from

its clip and fixed the lanyard to his right wrist. Carter
levelled with him and he mobilised every gramme of
energy in a thrust that lifted the heavy plate in a single, smooth swing. As he sensed it pass the point of
balance, he was up after it, head and shoulders
through the gap as it thudded to a stop against the
wall.

A Megaronian was facing him. Four metres off.
Hands flat on a desk top, half out of a swivel chair,
mouth open as the unexpected jammed his computer
with sudden queries. There were no answers. Koenig's
laser swept into aim and a stun beam filled his head
with an instant cloud of unknowing.

Caked with dust and sweat, with the glaring eye of
the lamp still fixed on his headband, the Alphan was
no bonus to see at the end of a duty stint. A man and a
girl walking towards a door in the wall behind the operator swung round to see what was happening to
Alan Carter fairly hurled himself out of the trap.

Two one-eyed trogs, materialising out of the par-
quet, were two too many for the girl. Hands to her
mouth, she was already buckling at the knees as Carter sprayed round with a wide angled beam.

There was no one else on the set. Leaving her
black-uniformed companion to fall where nature's
laws directed, Carter caught her neatly before she
reached the deck and sat her against a filing cabinet,
knees bent, chin on her hands, eyes open and still full
of horror.

There were two doors. One led to a circular landing and an elevator trunk. This was the one the two
had been making for. The other door was sealed and
carried a legend which Karl read off: "No Entry.
Spadec Directive One. Maximum Penalty."

Koenig said, "Watch the door, Karl. There could
be another one to come on duty."

So far so good, but there was no obvious way to
make the power switch. All the hardware in sight
seemed to be for distributing the incoming power for
local use. He crossed to the closed door and used his

vibrator to sheer out a panel round the lock. When it was open, he knew he was home and dry. Massive switchgear on one wall was marked up with pictographs that showed a spacer in a silo.

The rest of the room was filled by a huge computer spread. Across its front panels was the acronym spelled out in full: Social, Political And Defence Executive Computer.

Outside, there was the noise of an elevator tripping its stop and then a scuffle of feet as Carter brought in a plump girl in a grey caftan to sit beside her compatriot.

Koenig appeared in his doorway. "Fix the elevator, Alan. Then jam the door. What do we have? Two hours? A duty tour would not be less. So we can be back before the chase gets under way. But how do we make sure they don't reverse what we've done?

"Does it matter, if we get the silo open?"

"I'd like Victor's opinion on that, but I'd say not."

He would also have liked his scientific adviser to be there present and looking at Spadec. How far had the executive computer gone solo and how far was it still responsive to suggestions from the top brass in Caster? Were they as trapped by the system as everybody else, or were they still able to make programme changes?

Standing still and letting his mind take a run at it, he came up with the view that Spadec was the oracle in the cave. Even if it did not initiate policy, it was the ultimate director. The council framed a question, Spadec came up with the answer in line with a detailed programme, which had been stored in its memory in the long-distant past. By this time, nobody could break out of the circle, and for many, the will to do so was long gone.

Koenig checked the input. There was a land line and there was provision for a radio link. Even as he sorted it out, a relay dropped and lights flashed along the panels as somebody called in for advice. What was asked and what was answered was all kept inside

Spadec's head. But it had come in on a frequency in the band used by the air cars.

Two channels were operational. The land line—which would be the civil link for day-to-day government—and the military command link. There was a third, switched to 'Non Op," and Koenig called Karl to read the legend.

Karl said, "It is not easy, Commander. This is the ancient tongue. But as far as I can understand it, this would override all other input circuits. It is for emergency use, when a single control might be needed. Special instructions from this source would be prefaced by the key word 'omega.' "

Koenig shifted a cover plate and considered the circuitry. He was conscious that time was not on his side, but he cleared his mind of every other factor and went to work methodically. He had to leave it so that any quick inspection would not show that an adjustment had been made. When he replaced the panel, the switch for the third channel was still switched to "Non Op," but the link was open and set to respond on fourteen-twenty, which would please Sandra Benes, for one.

Alan Carter was hovering on the threshold. "We should move out, Commander."

"I know it."

Koenig turned to the massive switchgear for the power cable, heaved down the contact makers and spun rheostats to bring the distant silo on stream. Then he used his laser to weld the levers in place. It would take time to stop the flow.

He closed the hatch to Spadec's command post and used parts of the lock he had cut away to weld the door to its frame and melted the hinges for good measure. They would need a blowtorch to get inside.

Five minutes later, they had reached the trolley and were rocking away down the slope on the homeward leg.

The time lag was the weakest part of the exercise. Koenig was conscious of it. He reckoned that, at the best hope, there would be action in the power house at about the same time that they arrived at the silo. After that, it was anybody's guess as to how long it would take for the security outfit to reverse what he had done.

What was crystal clear, for a start, was that they should open the silo, without waiting for a full refuelling cycle. But then they were vulnerable and any air-car pilot with a kamikaze bent could home in on *Phoenix* and wreck the lift-off.

It was a delicate balance of bad choices. Koenig suspended judgement and pumped grimly at the see-saw lever. The argument was taken up below conscious level, where the holographic web of the human mind lived its own peculiar life. When a thread of light separated out at the end of the long conduit, a decision surfaced as though it had been inevitable all along. There was only one way to play it. They would open the silo and blast off with the best fuel load they could pack in before Caster got a full-scale strike organised. For that matter, they owed it to those who would stay behind. The four Outfarers and Cydon should have a chance to close the door behind them and seal off the rock as an unbreachable sanctuary.

Cydon's minimum working lights had been impressive enough. When they reached the silo the great pit was glowing with a new brilliance. *Phoenix* was soaking up power like a greedy sponge.

Koenig, tired as a dog, but driving himself, went straight to the control bunker. Bergman left the command desk and met him. "You did it, John."

"So far so good."

"I have Alpha standing by."

"Fuel?"

"There's a crash programme. As soon as the full power came on, I switched to it. Halves the time."

"So where are we now?"

"Thirty percent on board."

"What do we need?"

"For lift-off—a minimum of twenty percent. Full thrust to clear Megaron's gravisphere—another ten percent. Kano's been running some calculations. He reckons we need to maintain full thrust to match the Moon's speed and claw back some distance."

"Forty percent would give us a chance?"

"Fifty would be better. Sixty would be safe to break into Eagle range. We'd need the full hundred to land *Phoenix* on the Moon's surface."

"That's not on. But she would be no more than a museum piece anyway. We couldn't refuel her from Alpha. I'll talk to Main Mission. Meanwhile, open the lid and clear *Phoenix* for launch, while we have the power."

Koenig sat at the communications desk. The familiar Space Corporation call sign glowed on a blue background on the screen. He said, "Commander Koenig calling Main Mission," and the sign winked out. Sandra Benes, tuned meticulously to make a composition, with her chocolate-milk eyes on the upper Golden Section, said, "Commander?"

It was like rubbing a lamp and getting a beautiful genie, Koenig felt a surge of optimism. If he had been nearer, he would have been moved to pat her sleek head. He said, "Sandra, there's a computer down here that's gotten too big for its pedestal feet. I've set an override to respond on fourteen-twenty. I want a signal probe, with all the power you can give it, to trigger it off. They put me through on a link, so that I can talk to it through Alpha."

He might have been asking for a spoon to stir his coffee. Her "Check, Commander" suggested that she had hoped he would ask for something really difficult. For a count of five, he could only see the top of her head. Then she looked up. "Go ahead, anytime you like, Commander."

"Thank you, Sandra. Keep it open."

Helena Russell threw up a scan of the space centre on a wall screen. Light levels were falling. Cars were

drawn up beside the rock with two in the air making
patrol circuits, in case there was another exit from the
burrow and the Alphans broke cover.

Bergman said, "All set to open, John."

"Go ahead."

Helena looked at him and he knew what she was
thinking. There was another figure to watch the
screens. Cydon materialised by the hatch and walked
in.

"You are impatient, Commander."

"Tell me. Are there any defensive weapons to protect *Phoenix,* when the silo is open?"

"None. I have told you. The base was designed for
peaceful uses. The scientists here would have pre-
vented war, if they could have."

Karl and the rest of the party had come into the
bunker. All eyes were on Helena's screen, as Bergman activated the opening mechanism. Lights
dimmed, as power switched to the load. In the distant
town of Caster, citizens stopped in the streets as light
levels dropped to a glimmer.

There was a rumbling in the silo and a vibration
that shook the floor in the bunker. A slit appeared in
the huge dome, and widened as the two great
segments retracted into their housing. Then it was
done and the lights brightened, sending a yellow column into the gathering dusk.

The two patrolling cars changed course and ran in
to check this new phenomenon. Others began to rise
from the apron. Koenig began to talk to Alpha and
through Alpha to Spadec. He said, "This is Spadec
directive omega one. You will disregard all Spadec
instructions other than this. All previous commands
are null and void. When you hear this, you are free.
You are on your own. Your life is your own. Your
mind is your own. You are free to act in any
way which is human and reasonable. Any future
Spadec instruction will be false. The Social Political,
and Defence Computer has done its work and pre-
served you from many problems over the long years.

But now that work is done. It is time for you to wake from your long sleep and see what is done in your name. Be active, meet, talk, discuss your problems. Life is not easy. It is not meant to be easy. Living is struggling. You must learn to like it. There are great rewards. Make the future of Megaron equal in greatness to her past. As a symbol of renewal, a great ship, built by your ancestors, will be launched in a bid for the stars. Watch her and know that she bears the message of your ancient thinkers: "wisdom shall rise again.'"

Impulsively, Rhoda ran to him and put her arms round his neck. She said, "Thank you, Commander. Now I know I shall be happy on Alpha. You are a good people. Your visit to Megaron will be a turning point. Perhaps it was ordained, as I believe it was ordained that I should meet Alan."

They watched the screen. All the cars were airborne and circling the rock, nosing in to look at the brilliantly lit silo and then turning off to circle again. But the overall impression they gave was more of curious moths round a flame, than aggressive hawks looking for a place to strike.

Cydon said, "That was well done, Commander. I must revise my opinion of Earth Planet and of military men. You have struck at the mind and not the body. Who knows? Those who stay with me may witness great changes, sooner than I had dared to hope."

Not one to find compliments easy to take, Koenig said, harshly, "Nevertheless, when we have gone, you must close the silo again and stay watchful, until you are sure of a change of heart in Caster. There are some who went beyond the call of duty in Spadec's interests. True democracy may not suit all tastes. Things could go worse, before they get better. Even the Outfarers had their dissidents."

Koenig allowed an hour by the clock and found time to take a shower and eat a quick Passover meal with Cydon and the four Megaronians, who were to remain on the rock. As the time for embarkation neared, Rhoda went quiet. As they filed out to the gantry, Helena fell in beside her.

"What is it Rhoda?"

"I ask myself if I am doing the right thing."

"In what sense? For Alan or for you?"

"For Alan. Will I fit into your world? Are there differences between us which will make him unhappy?"

"Nobody can legislate for the long term, Rhoda. Forever is a long time. We all change. Hopefully, two people, who love each other, change in the same direction. But love is love and there isn't a great deal of it to be had in the universe. The Alphans will accept you and like you. You have three friends already, plus Alan, who is a loyal and honest man. There are not many like him, anywhere."

"For me, there is nobody like him."

"Well then. I don't think you need my opinion; but for what it's worth, I give it to you. If you stay, you will live with regret. If you come with us, you will share our dangers, but you will share our hopes. Even at that simple level, there is no real choice. You have to come."

The glow of conviction even endured when Carter strapped her into an acceleration couch in the rest cabin, before taking his own place on the command island. Golden eyes looked at him gravely through the visor of a space suit. He tapped the plexiglass with his gauntlet and breathed heavily into her outside mike. He said, "Don't go away and I'll be back as soon as we're in the clear."

He was gone and she was left with her memories of leave-taking and a miniature scanner to show her the gantry, where Karl, Gelanor, Urion and Hepa stood with the shadow figure of Cydon. They waved and withdrew to the bunker and its hatch slammed with a definitive thump, to mark the end of an era.

Koenig called for reports.

"Navigation?"

Carter answered, "Navigation. All systems go, Commander."

"Power?"

Bergman answered, "Power. All systems go, Commander."

"Communications?"

Helena Russell, the least sure, in an unfamiliar slot, managed an even tone. "All systems go, Commander."

Koenig rapidly cleared his desk in a sequence that brought the firing pin alive. A muted pinger on orchestral A sounded through the ship. As he heaved down the lever for a full due, a sweep hand began to count down.

As he waited, he reckoned he could have brought his people to strap themselves in on a bomb. Any one of a hundred systems could fail and anchor *Phoenix* in a pit that would turn into an inferno. The pinger cut out. There was a second of utter silence and stillness, as though they had dropped to the still point of the turning world, and then a trembling vibration beat the deep-foam insulation of the acceleration couches.

The watchers in the bunker heard the roar as the motors began to deliver. They saw streams of vermilion and cadmium-yellow flame jet from the tubes and break in a rolling surge along the blast trenches. The rock itself was vibrating under the savage storm of power that *Phoenix* was hurling into the foundations.

Then she was rising, slowly at first, jacking herself a metre at a time through the maze of gantries, until her gleaming cone was thrusting out into the darkening sky. Her immense length crept from the silo, as though there would be no end.

Suddenly an air car broke from the circling squadron. It had finally gotten home to Mestor that the Alphans had taken him all the way. His occupation was gone. Rage burned out all thought of Spadec instruction omega one. He pushed his pilot aside. Teeth set and eyes bleak, he aimed the air car for the shining tower that was materialising out of the rock.

Koenig saw the move and knew for a truth he could do nothing to stop it. Thumping the console with a bulky fist, he willed *Phoenix* to rise.

She was accelerating, even as Mestor started the run in. The great bird at her waist levelled with the rim of the silo, glowing crimson in the Promethean fire below. She hurled herself from her long resting place, as though eager to reach her true home in the interstellar wilderness.

Mestor had the emblem dead ahead and the car was roaring in on full power. Then it had gone and he was plunging forward into the incredible brilliance of the fireball. It was so quick, that the watchers in the bunker could hardly remember whether they had seen anything or not. One second, the black car was arrowing over the rock. The next it was gone, reduced to molecular trash, as though it had plunged into the surface of the Sun.

Koenig called Moonbase Alpha.

"Phoenix to Main Misson. Do you read me?"

Sandra Benes appeared on the miniature screen on the communications desk. "Main Mission to *Phoenix*. Loud and clear. Go ahead, *Phoenix."*

"It's all yours. I'm giving you a link to on-board computers. Have Kano run the course data. Plot the RV as close to Alpha as he can make it."

Kano answered for himself, dark face a smiling mask. "Check, Commander. We have you hooked on a line. It's only a question of time."

Phoenix was a bobbin running on the thread spun by her computers and reeled in by Main Mission. After an hour, Koenig was sure enough of the ship and their ability to handle her to call a stand down.

He switched all functions through to the command desk and set the rest of the crew free to gather in the ward room and see what the galley had to offer.

Carter made his way to the rest area. Rhoda was lying with her eyes closed and he squatted beside the acceleration couch, with his visor hinged away, watching her. She looked very young and very vulnerable, eyelashes in even arcs, dark hair piled in the crown of her helmet. He tapped the glass and her eyes flicked open. Emotional response to the pressures of mounting G had intensified the gold flecks. He reckoned soberly that human evolution was as surprising as any marvel in the universe. They considered each other gravely. Finally he snapped open the seals and pushed back her visor. Her hair spilled down in a silky black tide. He cleared a swathe and kissed her forehead, all he could reach with the bulky clutter of gear separating them.

Tongue moistening her lips, she said, "I knew it was a mistake to let myself get strapped onto this couch. Any passing sailor can take advantage."

"Have there been many?"

"To be truthful, you're the first. What's going on? I didn't like the first bit. Does that happen often?"

"You ask too many questions for a junior crewman. Show a little respect for the navigator."

"All right, Captain. What's going on, then?"

He unclipped the straps and pulled her to her feet "This you will like. It's meal time. You can help Helena in the galley."

"Is that right? Even in space, the woman gets to work in the kitchen? I might and I might not. But I'd certainly like to talk with Doctor Russell."

Following her down the narrow companion, Alan Carter grinned to himself. She was resilient. She was nobody's hey you. She would be all right on Alpha.

Silver scarabs on a black-velvet pad, three Eagles were in line astern, boring in to the RV. Even Alan Carter's critical eye could find no fault, as they turned in a copy-book manoeuvre and began to pace *Phoenix*. Beyond them, Earth's moon was a pallid disk. It was incredible that they should be glad to see her.

Fuel gauges on *Phoenix* were nudging into the red quadrant as the leading Eagle sidled in for the transfer. It was another first for Rhoda, and Carter hooked her with himself on the line that snaked out to pick them from the main hatch.

Last to leave, Koenig set the onboard computers for a course change that would take the ship off at a tangent. There was no power to land her and he did not fancy leaving even the outside chance that she might make a tunnelling bid through the roof of Main Mission.

They watched her from the direct-vision ports of the Eagle's passenger module. By any standards, she was the most elegant piece of craftsmanship that any culture could boast. As she turned to pick up her new course, she presented the emblem at her waist. She would carry it on, into an infinity of time and space, the proud symbol of the human mind and the great statement of human aspiration.

Helena Russell touched Koenig's arm. He knew what she was thinking. He said, "I know. In a way, it's sad and in a way it's great."

"Where will she end?"

"Who knows? Drawn into some sun that her builders never dreamed of. Launched in flame and ending in flame. But in a way, it doesn't matter. It's what she stands for.

"Wisdom shall rise again?"

"Something like that."

They were closing with Earth's moon. They could pick out the metallic glint of the sprawling base. The Eagles were making their proving run on the approach lanes. In its way, it was a kind of homecoming.

In the travel tube that picked them up from the launch pad, Koenig counted the cost. It had been an expensive reconnaissance. Moonbase Alpha could not afford too many abortive missions of the kind.

He said, "Nothing to log, Victor, except experience."

"I wouldn't say that, John." Bergman held up a storage jar with a ventilated screw top.

"What have you got here?"

"If you recall, the briefing for the mission included

a sampling survey for new strains for the hydroponic spread. These are from Cydon's store. Intended to supply *Phoenix*. Very vigorous. It could turn out to be cheap at the price."

Koenig thought of the enclave on the rock, which had endured through the millenia and had finally shrunk to one frail old man and his electronic shadow. It was a warning. Alpha could go the same way. He knew he had to redouble their efforts. They had to break out of their confining shell or they would get to like their chains and that would be the beginning of the end.

He had told the Megaronians that living was struggling. He gave himself another shot of ancient wisdom. Do not emotionalise over experience. Life is one thing after another. Look for the next challenge. Alpha was far from finished yet. The quest was still on.